". . . I get so tired of hearing about parties, parties, parties all the time. Don't you?" Lindsay asked, looking at me intently.

I nodded. Well, part of that was true. I did get tired of *hearing* about parties all the time—ones that I was never invited to. But now all that was going to change. I smiled even more brightly at Lindsay and tried to ignore the voice that said I was being disloyal to my best friend.

Best Friend Blues

by Karle Dickerson

For Marta, Sandy, and Alison
Best friends for now and always

Cover photo by John Strange

Published by Willowisp Press, Inc.
401 E. Wilson Bridge Road, Worthington, Ohio 43085

Printed in the United States of America

10 9 8 7 6 5 4 3 2 1

ISBN 0-87406-319-1

One

HE was a dummy all right.
But there *was* something human about him. It was weird. My best friend, Beverly Hansen, thought it was his expression. His eyes were half-closed, his mouth turned upward in a wavy grin, and his shaggy grayish brown hair looked like a mop. That's because it was a mop.

"But why is a dummy sitting on our doorstep?" I asked, bewildered. It was a week into Christmas vacation. Bev and I had been bored that day. First we watched our favorite game show, "Treasure Trove," on TV. Then we read mystery books together. They're our favorites. We'd spent a while making each other friendship bracelets. Finally we rode our bikes around the neighborhood. When we returned to my house, we found this life-sized dummy propped against the door.

"Look, Lisa! It's your brother. It's supposed to be Ash!" Bev screamed, reading a note that had been attached to the grimy sweatshirt the dummy was wearing.

"Why do you say that?" I demanded.

"The cheerleaders from Richmond High must have done it," Bev deduced. "They made a dummy of Ash, get it?"

I glared at her. Bev makes the worst jokes sometimes.

She read from the note: " 'Ash Halloran, you're a joke. Grover's team is gonna choke!' " I guess they think Richmond's gymnastic team will beat Grover's at the meet."

"No way! Grover will never lose." I shook my head. Ash was only a junior at Grover High, but he was captain of the varsity gymnastics team because he was so good. Grover's gymnastic team was good, too. In fact, the team had a good shot at going to the state championships. Richmond High School didn't stand a chance.

I picked up the dummy. I no longer saw anything funny about it. It made me mad that anyone would do something like this to make Ash look dumb. He was my brother, so I could fight with him all I wanted. But don't let me catch anyone else putting him down.

"Come on," I said. "Let's go throw this

6

stupid thing away before Ash comes home and sees it. It might make him feel bad."

Bev brushed her shiny brown hair out of her eyes. "Are you kidding? How could Ash feel bad about anything? He's Mr. Popularity, captain of the varsity gymnastics team. He's got girls falling all over him. You think a dumb dummy could make *him* feel bad?"

I rolled my eyes at Bev as I dragged the dummy up our driveway and pitched him in the garbage. I knew it was pretty close to true what she said about Ash. But I also knew it was true that Bev had had a crush on my big brother for months, so she tended to exaggerate about him sometimes. And it wasn't an ordinary crush either. It was a major crush.

I could have told Bev that having a crush on a high-school guy when you were still in middle school was hopeless, but I never did. After all, she was my best friend, and had been ever since third grade. We'd been alphabetized next to each other for a couple of years by then. So we decided we'd better become friends.

"Popularity, that's what Ash has, all right. You know, we'd better figure out something quick if we're going to be anything even remotely resembling popular at Foothill

Middle School," I said, partly to get her off the subject of Ash. I got tired of being Mr. Popular's sister and hearing people talk about him all the time. It was semi-sickening.

At the mention of the word "Foothill," Bev stopped on the driveway and made a face registering both terror and disgust.

"Why, oh, why did our district have to run out of money in the middle of the school year? I don't want to transfer to a new school. It's so crazy," she wailed.

She was right. It was crazy. Right before Christmas vacation, the school officials had sent home a note saying that our school, Kemper Middle School, was closing down for good. So the students were divided up among some other nearby middle schools. Starting in January, the beginning of the new semester, everyone is going to a new school. Next week.

"How will we ever make friends now? Breaking into the social order at a new school midyear is impossible," Bev went on.

"It's not fair," I muttered. "We were doing so well at Kemper. We had a lot of friends. Almost everyone knew who we were there. Now—*whammo!* We have to start all over again."

I knew it was going to be especially hard on Bev. She was pretty shy. Well, so was I, but not as shy as Bev. Last year, at the GATS (that's the Gifted and Talented Students group) assembly, my stomach turned to instant pudding when I had to go onstage to get my reading award. But I did it. As for Bev, well, she threw up backstage. Someone else had to go and get her award for her.

"Come on," I said. "We'd better get over to the Youth Club and help my mom so maybe she'll let us sunbathe at the pool today." Although it was December, this was Southern California. And Decembers can get pretty hot sometimes, like today. I hoped Mom would open up the pool area for us, even though there was no water in the pool itself. Mom's the director of the Youth Club, so she can do things like open up the pool.

Bev's green eyes flashed dangerously. "I know why you want to go today. It's because you're hoping Brendan MacIntyre will be at the Youth Club. Doesn't he have guitar lessons today?" I gave Bev my killer look. Brendan had danced *one dance* with me at the Youth Club holiday dance, and Bev had been bugging me about him ever since.

"How should I know?" I shrugged. I didn't want Bev to know that I even remotely thought Brendan was cute, or she'd tease me forever. So now I was trying to throw her off track by pretending I didn't care. At least Brendan would be going to Foothill too.

A couple of hours later, we were sunning ourselves by the pool. Unfortunately, Brendan was nowhere in sight. I guess he had better things to do. Rats.

"You know, Bev, I really think we'd better figure out a social strategy for the new school this year," I said as I smeared a generous blob of zinc oxide on my nose. "Otherwise, we could get left out of everything at Foothill."

"Maybe you're right," she sighed as she glopped on sunscreen that smelled like tropical fruit. "Eighth grade is the year that matters. At least, that's what Ash says. And he should know."

"Popularity. That's all that matters," I said strongly.

"What about being good students?" asked Bev.

"We already *are* good students," I pointed out. "We've won every reading award known to mankind. Then we have our red ribbons from the science fair last year. Now all we need is to make sure we break into the right social groups at Foothill."

"Yeah," Bev said. "I want people at Foothill to know how wonderful and brilliant we are."

"What can we do?" I continued. "Foothill's

so huge. We don't know any of the popular kids there. Except for Lori Pendleton and Maria Perez," I said thoughtfully. I was referring to a couple of definitely in-crowd girls we knew who often hung around the Youth Club.

"I swear, girls like that are born with 'Best-Dressed Eighth Grader' and 'Girl With Cutest Smile' pasted on their birth certificates," Bev chimed in mournfully. "We need something to capture some attention."

"Why don't teachers hand out popularity manuals when you first come to a new school? Most kids would rather read a popularity guide than those dumb ones about school rules," I said. I was wishing Bev would come up with a good idea because I sure couldn't.

I kept talking along those lines for a while. But soon I noticed Bev had shoved a wadded-up towel over her head. This was a good sign. She probably wanted to snuff out the sound of my voice because she was cooking up an idea.

I shouted, "We'll be doomed," to give Bev a little encouragement.

It worked. She sat up and threw off her towel dramatically. "I've got it! We can make a manual of our own. A Social Survival Guide! We'll collect data on popularity.

"We can get case studies, interview popular guys and girls. It'll be easy. Then, good-bye to

11

new-girl status! Hello, popularity!" Bev's face glowed. It always did whenever she came up with a brilliant idea.

"Oodles of popular friends," I shouted, hugging myself, my head swimming with enticing possibilities. "Eating at the right tables at lunch!"

"I can see it now," exclaimed Bev. "Picture the yearbook: Lisa Halloran and Beverly Hansen—Most Popular Eighth Graders!"

And so that's how the Social Survival Guide came to be. Whenever we had a spare moment from helping my mom set up for the New Year's Eve party down at the Youth Club, Bev and I put the Guide together. To the eye, it didn't look like much. It consisted of a notebook and some magazines.

But inside the notebook were the secrets we were sure would make us successful. Bev and I had looked through every teen magazine around. We jotted down fashion and beauty ideas in our red spiral notebook. We listened to the hit radio station faithfully so we'd be up on the latest groups and songs. We did extensive observation at the Youth Club where tons of kids gathered together during vacation.

By New Year's Eve, our notes were pretty complete. Then we spent a day or so organizing our findings. We emptied our closets and ruthlessly weeded out any articles of clothing we even suspected of being out of it. These went into the charity bag, with our parents' permission. Finally, we set to work on the final touch.

This was the fun part. We convinced my parents and Bev's dad to let us spend some of our Christmas money. This way, we could invest in our immediate futures. Then we set off for the mall to outfit ourselves. First we raided the juniors' departments of only the trendiest stores. We each bought new jeans. Then we had makeovers done by those overly made-up ladies at the makeup counters. Of course, all we bought was some new mascara and light lip gloss—the only makeup our parents would let us wear.

The day before our dazzling entrance at our new school, we were back at the Youth Club cleaning up the rest of the holiday decorations. "Well, tomorrow's the day," I said to Bev.

"Lisa, do you think all this was worth it?" asked Bev, nervously twiddling with a string of lights we were stuffing into a box.

"No problem. We've covered everything," I answered confidently. "We're up on the latest groups and music videos. We both have new jeans, new makeup, new haircuts, new everything. Well, almost. Are you sure you can't convince your dad to let you get contact lenses?"

"No way. But I hope you're right. I think we have the rest of it covered," sighed Bev.

"It's simple. All we have to do is get people to notice us. Talk to everybody who's somebody even if you can't stand them. And for heaven's sake, smile no matter what," I said. "Right now, that shouldn't be too hard. Here comes my brother."

Bev merely squealed and hid behind a stack of boxes. That was dumb because it wasn't like she didn't see Ash nearly every day. She'd never learn to stop being shy. Would our Social Survival idea ever get off the ground?

Two

THE next morning, Bev and I met at my house so we could walk together to the bus stop to face our first day at Foothill. Ash sped off in his used Trans Am that my parents bought for him for his sixteenth birthday.

Bev and I looked on jealously. But then I decided we had to concentrate our thoughts on the matter at hand.

"Today's the day," I declared grimly.

"Does my hair look too wild?" asked Bev nervously. She must have put a whole container of hairspray on it.

"No, you look fine," I said. She did. I always thought Bev had hope in the looks department. Not like me. People said I was cute, but all I saw was plain, plain, plain. No getting around it, I was the steady, dependable-looking type. Yuck. I wanted to look captivating and unpredictable.

"Does this shirt make my eyes look green?" I asked hopefully.

"Nope," answered Bev a little too truthfully for my taste.

I sighed and we began our walk to the bus stop.

Unfortunately, our first day at Foothill was nothing more than an endless round of new GATS classrooms. And I mean nothing more. Worse yet, Bev and I didn't have a single class together. Finding out that Brendan was in my history class was the only thing that went right all day.

You see, even though Bev and I hoped we looked like Very Important Students, apparently the Foothill kids didn't think that much of us. In fact, I don't think they thought about us at all. In spite of our trendsetting clothes and smiles that lit up like high beams on a car, no one important said more than a soggy-cereal "hi" to me or Bev.

"They'll notice us soon," said Bev hopefully as we rode home on the school bus.

By the second day of school, however, I could see that we needed to go for the heavy artillery. With almost a thousand students roaming those halls, it was going to take more than carefully chosen clothes, cute smiles, or even a half-formed Social Survival Guide to make a dent in this school.

"I've got it!" I screeched to Bev while we toyed with the mini-sundaes we'd treated ourselves to at an ice-cream shop after school.

"Got what?" Beverly said, eyeing me warily. When the ideas weren't hers, she always seemed a little suspicious.

"We can't go this alone. We need a guide! Why didn't we think of that before?" I asked, slapping my hand to my forehead.

Beverly merely resumed scraping her sundae cup for any final survivors of her nibble attack.

"We need to find a popular girl at Foothill who knows her way around school and who's willing to share her secrets with us. Foothill is a bigger beast than I thought!"

My mind moved ahead. The first problem, of course, was finding a popular girl who'd talk to us. The second problem was convincing whoever-she-might-be to part with hard-won popularity pointers.

Bev carefully licked her spoon, then said, "I'm not sure we need a guide. We just need to give it time."

"We've given it enough time. If we wait much longer, we'll doom ourselves to oblivion," I stated flatly. "Could you stand it if the high point of eighth grade was the end-of-the-year science club banquet? We could go all year and never once be invited to a single party."

"Oh, by the way, do you like Ms. Penney?" Bev asked, referring to the new science teacher she had first period and I had sixth.

"Oh, she's all right. But we've never had problems getting along with teachers. What we need to worry about is getting the Foothill crowd to like us," I said. Then I got up to throw away my sundae cup. "Come on, let's go over to the Youth Club and see what's going on there."

"I think I'll head home instead and get started on my book report for English," Bev said, still peering inside her cup hopefully.

"Okay," I said, then picked up my books and started off for the Youth Club. Sometimes Bev and I helped my mom out, but more often we played ping-pong or watched the little kids. Bev's mom died when she was a baby, so she sort of adopted my mom. It's fine with me. Mom and I don't always get along, but she has a lot of love to go around.

"Is that you, Punkin?" Mom called as I walked through the front door of the Youth Club. She was sitting at her computer. "I'm in here working on the kids' musical program. What's up?"

I shrugged. "Nothing."

"So, listen, Punkin," Mom said, frowning at her computer. "Will you help me out with the musical this year? I'll need a few more kids to help out, too. We're doing a program called *I Love Me.* The children are going to learn about self-esteem. I really need it to be a big success. Or I can kiss the budget good-bye."

"Sure," I said with a shrug. Last year the program had been called *Safety Kids.* It was designed to teach kids to act responsibly about personal safety. I had helped. I'd really enjoyed working with the four- to eight-year-olds. But since I had some hang-ups in the love-myself department, I wasn't sure if I could help little kids sing about loving themselves. Mom didn't say anything else, so I decided not to bug her with questions. I walked out back near the tennis courts toward my favorite bench.

Well, guess what? Brendan MacIntyre also had chosen that place to sit down and study. He looked up at me. Rats. I wished he hadn't seen me. I was sweaty and tired and looked awful. But it was too late to duck back in the door and go study somewhere else.

"Hi, Lisa," Brendan said. He shoved his stuff over to make room for me.

"Hi." I sat down next to him, praying he

wouldn't notice how I looked.

"Hey, what are you and Bev doing for the science project this year?" he asked.

Actually, I hadn't planned to do one this year, so I shrugged. I stole a few looks at the way Brendan's dark, curly hair wisped around his ears as he turned back to his books. A minute later, he caught me looking at him and we were locked eyeball-to-eyeball for a moment. Embarrassed, I frantically grabbed my notebook for some paper. I wished I wasn't a total clod around guys.

Just then, Lori Pendleton walked by with a group of kids holding tennis rackets. Lori was also holding the hand of this cute guy from Foothill named Jason Johansen. As they passed us, they laughed at some shared joke. I swallowed a lump of despair. Would I ever feel like I really belonged to a cool-looking group like that?

Three

AFTER second period the next day, Bev and I met at our shared locker.

"The usual place for lunch?" I asked, shoving in my history book.

"Huh-uh," said Bev, shaking her head. "The science club meets during lunch hour. Room 216. You're coming, aren't you? Brendan is joining."

"Big deal," I said. *So that's why he asked about our project,* I thought. Still, even for Brendan I wasn't going to give up my lunch hour—the prime hour to scout for just the right popular crowd to hook up with.

"Guess what I heard? The state science fair is being held at Disneyland this year. And it's never too early to start thinking about getting in on that. You should come to the meeting. Everyone liked our chicken embryo project last year," Bev reminded me.

"Big deal. So we won a red ribbon at the science fair. You're forgetting a more important thing—our Social Survival Guide," I reminded Bev sharply. "We need to take some new notes."

"I guess you're right. The Guide as it is definitely isn't helping," Bev said as she slammed the locker. "No one here at Foothill even acknowledges that I exist. I smiled at everyone till my mouth went numb this morning, and no one noticed. I don't think anyone would look twice if I were dancing on top of the lockers with a six-foot python wrapped around my neck."

"So can't you forget science club just for today so we can work on it?" I wailed pathetically. I thought I'd resort to my old guilt ploy as a last-ditch effort.

It didn't thaw her cold heart a single degree. She knew me too well.

"Eat with somebody else," Bev said unsympathetically. "Since you won't come, I'll meet you after school."

So there I was at lunchtime, sitting on the wall that went around the patio by the library. I nibbled half-heartedly on a semi-stale turkey sandwich and bag of corn chips. In between bites, I watched some popular kids hanging out on the lawns nearby, catching the sun.

Since the winters are never fierce here, Foothill was laid out like many Southern California schools. All the classrooms opened to the outside, and they were surrounded with grassy courtyards.

I didn't want to be a snob or anything, but I knew that deciding whom to hang out with was a BIG issue. I mean, sitting at the wrong table or patch of lawn could ruin me!

Right as the warning bell rang, my big brother Ash walked by with his pal Ryan and some of his friends. Grover High School is practically next door to Foothill. I guessed they slipped off school grounds to go to the Burger Palace, where some kids hang out during lunch.

I knew Ash would sooner die than acknowledge his miniscule middle-school sis, but a couple of the guys with him nodded and grunted *hi's* to me. Ryan winked and tossed me the football the group had been passing back and forth.

"How's it going, Lisa?" he called as he spiraled the ball in my direction.

"Oh, it's going, all right," I said with a lilt, like I'd heard some of the high-school girls do. Then I giggled. It didn't sound like me, but there must be something to it if other girls did it.

23

Of course, the only reason he paid any attention to me was because I was related to Ash, but all the same, I could see a couple of the "cool crowd" girls, including one very pretty blond I didn't know, look my way enviously.

If only Bev could see me now. Well, that's what she got for deserting me in my hour of need for some dumb club meeting. I kept my cool and caught the ball nonchalantly. Then I threw it back, acting as if I always had high-school guys hanging around me.

Ash and his friends walked on, and I scooped up my books, ready to run across the lawn to the far bungalows where my Spanish class was. I had just enough time to dart into the girls' room where some popular kids hung out. I ran past a group of them who were talking and laughing under a big shade tree next to the entrance of the girls' room.

Unfortunately, the restroom was so jam-packed with a zillion other girls, I had to wait for a place in front of the mirror. I was just about to leave, when suddenly I was aware of the poppity-pop-pop sounds of a motor coming closer. Funny—the parking lot was on the other side of the grounds.

My eyes caught those of a tall, red-headed girl in the mirror. She was expertly applying sweeps of eyeshadow.

"That sounds like Lindsay Sparks," she said.

"Who's Lindsay Sparks?" I asked.

"You don't know who Lindsay Sparks is? You're probably the only person who doesn't. She's new here because she got kicked out of private school. Her mom—" The sounds of the motor came closer yet, drowning out any further conversation.

The sound grew deafening. I spun around and stared down at the front wheel of a shiny red motor scooter. It nudged its way into the door of the restroom. I looked incredulously at the advancing wheel for a second, then jumped back as a pretty blond girl steered the scooter—inside the room!

The girl leaned over and with polished fingernails, switched off the key. I must have been staring, because she pursed her lips and sat there staring at me for a moment before speaking.

"What's the matter with you? Never seen a scooter before?" she asked coolly.

It was incredible how Lindsay Sparks just sort of seemed to fill up the room. For one thing, she looked like she belonged on the cover of a teen magazine with her soft good looks. She was wearing a fuzzy peach sweater over tight white pants, and large silver earrings framed the fine bones of her face.

I recovered quickly. "Of course," I declared hotly. "It's just not too often I've had to step over one in the girls' bathroom."

"Hi, Lindsay," interrupted the red-haired girl. "I hope you're going with the gang to Skip Steinman's party tonight. Everyone's going to be there. Well, I've got to run," she said as she inched past the scooter and dashed out. Then the tardy bell rang. I stood there, playing eyeball ping-pong between the door and Lindsay. Should I bolt to class or stay and try to talk to her? Somehow, my legs just wouldn't carry me out of the bathroom.

"Hey, aren't you friends with Ryan McCarron?" Lindsay asked, looking at me with a sharp look.

"Uh," I managed. I suddenly recognized Lindsay as the beautiful blond who'd watched my football toss with Ryan at lunch. From a distance I guess it could have looked like Ryan and I were friends.

"Do you also know that cute Ash Halloran?" Lindsay asked.

"He—he's my big brother," I stammered. Why couldn't I speak? "What are you doing in here on that thing anyway?" I added, trying to think of something to say.

"Well, I usually have better places to go than into girls' rooms," Lindsay said, gesturing as if that explained the presence of the scooter. "But I was running late, and I knew I'd find someone in here. Everyone else was charging around because of the bell, and I needed to find someone who'd lend me the textbook I need for my next class. I see you've got it."

I followed her heavily fringed green eyes to my stack of books resting on the shelf under the mirror.

"Lend me the book of short stories," she said sweetly with a wide smile that revealed straight white teeth. It was definitely a command.

Without even considering that I'd need it that afternoon, I gave her the book. Then, I didn't know why, but I burst into giggles.

I think it was just the ridiculousness of the situation. There I was, mesmerized by a mysterious girl on a motor scooter in the girls' bathroom, and ready to give up my English book. Wait till I tell Bev! This seemed like a scene right out of one of our favorite mystery novels.

Lindsay looked at me questioningly.

"I'm sorry," I sputtered. "I wasn't laughing at you. It's just that . . . that . . . I mean . . . " I tried to explain about the mystery novels, but Lindsay just gave me this weird look.

After a moment, Lindsay's face broke into an honest-to-goodness grin, and she said, "Hey, are you new here? Oh, you must be one of those new transfer kids—well, never mind. Come on. Hop on the back of my bike. I'll take you to your class." She leaned over and turned the key and the deafening roar started once again.

There didn't seem to be anything else to do but obey her. I grabbed the rest of my books and climbed on the back of the seat. I wondered how Lindsay could be so brave, breaking school rules by driving one of these things. I wondered if I could be arrested as an accomplice.

We backed out the door of the girls' room, and then Lindsay pushed down on the throttle. I desperately held on tightly to the sides of the seat while we careened down the walkway. "Where to?" Lindsay called as an afterthought, her light blond hair whipping into my mouth.

"The bungalows. Room 302. Mr. Morris' class," I shouted back.

"Oh, you have Gary, huh? He's soooo cute!" she shouted. I didn't answer. I'd never heard of anyone calling a teacher by his first name before.

We pulled up outside the room. Whew! I was still alive. Lindsay gave me a little wave and a dazzling smile. "Meet me after school by the library and I'll return your book. Thanks, and tell Gary I said a special hello," she called and sped off.

I straightened my hair, readjusted my books and steeled myself to walk into Spanish class. I knew everybody had noticed my arrival, and I was late to boot. I hoped I wouldn't get detention for the rest of my life.

The door screeched as I swung it open, and thirty pairs of eyes turned toward me. But all Mr. Morris said was, "Was that Lindsay Sparks?" He threw me an indulgent look as I nodded sheepishly and slunk to my seat.

While the rest of the class conjugated irregular verbs, I sat in a dizzy whirl thinking about Lindsay. She sure had some power. During a film about the Aztecs that Mr. Morris flicked on midway through the class, I thought more about Lindsay. People probably noticed her wherever she went—even without her motor scooter!

During the sacrificial rites scene in the film, something started clicking in my brain. If everyone noticed Lindsay, wouldn't they notice me if I was her friend? Maybe Lindsay was just the thing I needed to make the Social

Survival Guide work. Now . . . how would I arrange this friendship?

The answer came to me just minutes before the end of the period. Lindsay had seemed interested in Ash. Maybe, I could figure out a way to get Ash and Lindsay together! And in return, Lindsay could help me get the social start Bev and I needed at Foothill.

There were a couple of tricky things though. One was how would I get a high-school guy interested in a middle-school girl? The next problem—I couldn't count on Bev to help me hook up Lindsay with Ash. After all, she had that industrial-strength crush on Ash herself. I was on my own.

The rest of my afternoon classes went quickly. I didn't concentrate much in my classes since I was thinking about Lindsay and Ash.

That afternoon, Ms. Penney, the science teacher, asked me to stay after class. *Rats,* I thought to myself. She was probably going to corner me and ask me why I didn't come to science club that afternoon.

Sure enough, that's exactly what she did. When she was finally finished talking to me, I raced out to the front lawn. I had to get my book back from Lindsay. But I think I really just wanted to see her again to see if she'd just been a figment of my imagination!

Four

BEV was still waiting at our usual spot on the front lawn by the library, even though she missed the bus because of me. The weather had changed suddenly, and now a light rain was misting down on us. I'd just slipped on the slick walkway and skinned my knees. I hoped like crazy that nobody had seen me fall.

"Let's go. I'm freezing," Bev exclaimed, shivering and hugging her books to her chest. We were in for a long, miserable walk home.

"We can't go just yet. I need to find someone." I wondered if Lindsay would still be around. The way Bev looked at me I could tell she thought my brain cells had deactivated or something.

"Guess who I saw at lunch today?" I said mysteriously, trying to draw Bev's mind away from the uncomfortable reality of the rain.

"Ash!" I exclaimed, before she could guess. "He sneaked on campus with some friends, and he wanted to know where you were." Okay, so I lied about the last part, but the light mist was turning into fat droplets and Bev was getting annoyed.

"He did not," said Bev. "Come on. Let's go." The fat droplets were turning even fatter.

"I can't just yet," I said, feeling worried as I glanced at my watch. "I need to get my English book back from a girl I lent it to. She said she'd meet me here. I hope I didn't miss her."

After a few more minutes, I gave up. I guessed it didn't occur to someone like Lindsay to return things she borrowed.

"Well, I guess she isn't coming. Let's go. Sorry I kept you waiting," I said with a sigh.

Bev and I set out for our wet walk home, and on the way, I told her about meeting Lindsay on her motor scooter in the bathroom. I tried to play up Lindsay's thoughtfulness in offering me a ride back to class, but Bev was not impressed.

"If you want my opinion, this Lindsay sounds like a world-class jerk," she said, brushing a drop of rain off her nose when I finished.

"Are you kidding? Don't you get it?" I jabbered on excitedly, trying one last time to get

Bev excited over the Plan. At this point, I wasn't going to tell her about the Lindsay-Ash connection. "She's everything we need for our Social Survival Guide! She's pretty, totally unshy and it seems like everyone here knows her."

"I'm not sure that's such a big deal anymore," was Bev's only comment.

"What?" I asked. Bev was beginning to amaze me.

"I'm not impressed, Lisa. I think anyone who would swipe your book—"

"She borrowed it," I interrupted.

". . . who would *swipe* your book," Bev continued, "does not deserve to have you nominate her as Miss Wonderful Universe! She deserves to have her locker handle smeared with peanut butter as punishment."

I jumped in swiftly. "Hey, don't you dare do anything so embarrassing!"

"It was just a thought," Bev said defensively. "Are you worried it would upset your Lindsay friend?"

"Bev, are you jealous?" I asked.

"Get serious. Who else could stand being your best friend?"

"It isn't an easy job," I agreed, laughing. And instantly, I wasn't mad anymore. Bev and I had been friends for so long, we couldn't imagine what we'd do without each other. But of course, we couldn't admit this out loud. I decided for the sake of our friendship to drop the subject of Lindsay. And I didn't even pursue the Social Survival Guide. Instead, I told Bev that my mom could use some help with the Youth Club's yearly musical event.

"Sure!" said Bev. "Those kids are so cute—I like working with them. What are they doing this year?"

"Oh, something about self-esteem. The program's called *I Love Me*."

"Sounds neat." Then Bev sneezed. "By the way, what are we going to do for a science project?"

I didn't have the heart to tell Bev I'd made up my mind to skip the science fair this year, but we tossed around ideas for a project anyway. It was a long walk from Foothill, but we didn't come up with any ideas we both liked.

When we got to my house, I waved good-bye to Bev and walked up our bumpy, long driveway, which was filled with potholes brimming with rainwater.

I stepped inside the laundry room and dropped my drenched books on top of the washing machine. Then I made my way into the kitchen and opened the refrigerator. No luck. There was only some unidentifiable gross green stuff in a plastic container. Ash had beaten me home and practically cleaned the whole kitchen out.

"Ash, did you eat *all* the turkey?" I asked as Ryan strolled into the kitchen. I knew Ash couldn't be far behind.

"Yep," he called from the hallway. "Is it safe, Ryan? Can I come in?"

Ash came in the kitchen with an expression of exaggerated fear on his face. His eyes darted dramatically around the room like he was sure I was going to pounce on him.

"*And* half a loaf of bread?" I added, ignoring Ash's theatrics.

"Yep," Ash said again, and he patted his flat stomach. "And the rest of the cheese and a few cookies as well."

"Thanks, pig," I replied. "What am I supposed to eat?"

"Defrost something. Mom called and said she'd be home late from the Club, so you're supposed to make something for dinner anyway." Ash opened the freezer and studied the contents long and hard before pulling out a couple of packages of frozen chicken dinners. He unwrapped them and slid them into the microwave oven.

"There. You can have some chicken when it's done. Now wasn't that nice of me?"

"Thanks, Brother Mom," I quipped. "It's your turn to cook anyway since I did it last time." Actually, if the truth be known, Ash is the cook in our family. Mom hates to cook, and I'm hopeless. Ash and I take turns with dinner when Mom's late or out of town. His dinners are masterpieces, while mine are merely digestive disturbances.

"Aha! What have we here? Half of a sugar donut!" Ash crowed exultantly as he yanked open the bread drawer.

"It's mine," I shouted and tried to grab it. The donut fell to the linoleum and we both made a dive for it, giggling while we pushed each other away. The noise brought our two dingbat Welsh corgies scurrying in, yapping and snapping to join the fight. I emerged victoriously after tickling Ash viciously in the ribs.

"It's yours! Geez, you fight dirty for a girl." Ash laughed and surrendered, standing up and dusting himself off. "Shut up, Bertha and Bertie. Why do we have these little rats instead of real dogs anyway?"

"I love them," I yelled, even though I knew Ash was just saying that. He loved those dogs just as much as I did.

Ryan pulled out a chair and sat backward on it, his long legs stretched out in front of him.

He scratched the little dogs on the head and watched me down the donut.

I decided now was as good a time as ever to launch my plan.

"I've got news for you. I met a girl you'd probably be very interested in today." I tossed my hair back airily like I'd seen Lori Pendleton do. "Her name is Lindsay Sparks and she'd make both of your mouths hang open. She's got one of those neat motor scooters, and she rides it all over school."

Ryan's and my brother's eyes met. Then Ryan said, "Lindsay Sparks? Yeah, we've heard of her. She's Desirée Sparks' daughter. The game-show hostess on—what's it called? *The Treasure Trove*—or something like that."

I blinked. I knew, of course, who Desirée Sparks was. I'd been watching her show for years. But it had never occurred to me that Lindsay was her daughter. Desirée didn't look like the motherly type, that was for sure.

Well, that explained a lot of things. Like why everybody knew who Lindsay was and why she was so supremely confident. Desirée Sparks' daughter! Since we lived only over the hill from Hollywood in the San Fernando Valley, we were always hearing about TV and movie stars. But to actually know one! Well, the daughter of one, anyway.

"You know Lindsay?" I said weakly.

"No, but I read that Desirée Sparks was moving to Foothill in *The Valley Sheet* about a month ago," Ryan said, referring to our local newspaper. "In fact, they moved to Crescent Street into that big Tudor mansion that big oil-company guy used to own. I hear this Lindsay is gorgeous."

"She's good-looking all right," Ash agreed. I stared at Ash for a moment, my mental gears shifting into fast-forward. Aha! So Ash seemed interested in Lindsay too. I rolled that thought around in my mind while waiting for the chicken to cook.

Ash cut into my thoughts. "By the way, Mom says you're helping her with that little kids' sing thing. The rehearsals start in a couple of days. Think you can get some of your dinky friends to help out so I don't get stuck with all the work?"

I just glared.

"Okay, maybe I shouldn't have said that," Ash said. "I'll watch the chicken for you and put dinner together if you'll try to get some of your friends to help bail me out."

"I'll think about it," I said, giving in a little bit, since Ash was making an effort to be nice.

Then without thinking, I bent over to examine my skinned knees. They weren't bleeding anymore. I stood up.

"Oh, Lisa, Lisa, the girl of my dreams," Ryan started singing in this off-key voice to the tune of *The Treasure Trove* theme song. "My dream girl has scabby knees!"

I tried to sic Bertie and Bertha on him, but the dogs just gave me their usual confused looks. I gave up and ran upstairs to my bedroom, planning to examine my knees in a full-length mirror.

Instead, I grabbed *The Mystery of the Flickering Lamplight*. I couldn't help thinking that one of the main characters sounded just like Brendan. He was romantic and good-looking. I closed the book after a while. I pretended I knew guys who said things like, "Ah, 'tis you, my gentle flower," instead of "What's your science project this year?"

Five

I have the worst luck!

The next day, Bev's dad called me right before I left the house to tell me Bev had the sniffles and wouldn't be going to school. He added in his stern doctor's voice that he wasn't sure it had been a good idea for Bev to stand around waiting in the rain. Like it was all my fault that Bev had gotten a cold. Just as I was hanging up, Bertie and Bertha came in and jumped all over me.

"Get down, you monsters!" I barked. They barked back, as usual, their little claws scritching all over the hardwood floors as they frantically leaped on me.

I started off on my lonely walk to the bus stop, my feet dragging and my spirits flagging. I always felt kind of lonely when Bev was absent. Oh well, at least it gave me a chance to review the Social Survival Guide. I also had more than enough opportunity to wonder how I was going to get my book back before English class. When I got to school, I walked up to one group of popular kids I'd noticed the first day I'd come to Foothill.

"Excuse me," I said, my voice sounding wimpy even to me, "but have you seen Lindsay Sparks around anywhere yet?"

"Are you kidding? This early?" hooted one boy.

The rest of the kids merely looked me up and down in a cold, bored way. I got out of there in a hurry and went over to the bike racks to see if maybe Lindsay had parked her motor scooter. No luck. I finally gave up, then fought my way through the crowded halls to first period.

By second period, which was math, I had a first-rate stomachache coming on. I always get one when something upsets me. If I didn't find Lindsay by lunchtime and get my book back, I wouldn't have time to get my English homework done. Then I'd be in for real trouble. My English teacher, Mrs. Pierce, wasn't the type to accept excuses.

A minute later, it occurred to me where Lindsay might be. When the bell rang, I bolted out of the room and flew down the stairs past the pay phones outside to the girls' room.

Unfortunately, Lindsay wasn't there, but neither was anyone else. Oh well, it had been worth a try.

I turned to leave, but just then I heard the poppity-pop of a motor scooter. In roared Lindsay, giving me a strange half-smile. She was wearing a brilliant blue sweater with the cutest jeans skirt I'd ever seen.

"Looking for this?" Lindsay asked in a slightly bored voice, then tossed me my book. I caught it clumsily, noting that my neat new book cover had been torn off.

"Uh, thanks," I muttered.

"Oh, it was nothing," she replied lightly. "Turned out to be the wrong book anyway. I had to call up Marcia Brewer and talk William into driving over to borrow hers."

I wondered for a second who William was. Then I felt something rise to my throat—was it anger? I mean, why hadn't Lindsay checked first before she borrowed my book to see if it was the right one? Why hadn't she looked for me after school to return it to me? I could have done my assignment last night instead of sweating and getting a stomachache over the whole thing.

What I said instead was, "How did you know where to find me?"

Lindsay's silvery laugh floated around the

tiny room. "Huh? Oh, that was easy. I figured you'd be back here in the bathroom about this time."

I almost said something, but instantly changed my mind. *Remember the Plan,* I reminded myself. That calmed me down. I took a deep breath, then mentioned that my brother Ash watched her mom on TV whenever he got the chance. He didn't, of course. He hated TV, but I said it anyway. That got Lindsay's interest.

But before she had a chance to say anything—wouldn't you know it—Lori and Maria came in. They were giggling about someone, their heads close together. They looked right through me—what else?—but stopped abruptly when they saw Lindsay and stood closely around her. It was sort of like what Bertie and Bertha do whenever I'm eating something they want to scrounge.

"Hi, Lindsay," cooed Maria. "Oh, what a darling sweater! Where did you get it? Did your mom buy it for you?"

Lindsay shrugged and shook back her hair. Her large, dangly earrings glinted against the sweater. "This gross thing? Oh, at some little boutique on Rodeo Drive. Mother took me shopping last weekend."

"Wow! You shop on Rodeo Drive?" I cut in.

I wished my family could shop somewhere glamorous like Rodeo Drive. My mom nearly always got our stuff at month-end sales downtown.

I realized that Lori and Maria were now looking strangely at me. They were no doubt wondering why a star like Lindsay was bothering with an unknown like me.

"Are you going to Blake Martin's party Friday?" asked Lori, now looking at Lindsay. "We're going to have fun like you can't believe."

"Her brother's band is going to play," supplied Maria. "Even some cute guys from Grover are coming." It was like they were dangling bait for Lindsay to bite.

"Oh, I might. It all depends on if my mom wants to go to our beach house for the weekend or not," Lindsay replied. "You heading toward the drama wing? Let's get out of here," she said to me, turning away from the others.

I followed her out the door automatically. Wow! She actually chose to walk to class with me rather than to talk with Lori and Maria. I decided I could forgive her for a dozen missing book covers. Anyway, it wasn't like I didn't have more at home. Lindsay parked her scooter, and we headed across the lawn.

"Sometimes they make me crazy. I get so tired of hearing about parties, parties, parties all the time. Don't you?" Lindsay asked, looking at me intently.

I nodded. Well, part of that was true. I did get tired of *hearing* about parties all the time—ones that I was never invited to. *Well, that's going to change,* I reminded myself. I smiled even more brightly at Lindsay and tried to ignore the voice that said I was being disloyal to my best friend.

"Hey, you took some great notes in your English class, by the way," Lindsay said as we crossed the quad. I noticed she wasn't carrying any books. "I lent them to a friend of mine. I hope you don't mind."

How could I mind? I had all that stuff in my head anyway. English was one of my best subjects. Anyway, I was relieved to have my book back. I was also pretty happy that Lindsay preferred to talk to me instead of the other girls. Nothing she could have done would have made me terminally mad at that moment.

"No big deal," I answered. As we walked, I couldn't help noticing that a few of the kids I'd asked about Lindsay this morning turned their heads and really looked at me. The attention helped me overcome my shyness a little bit more, and I started to relax.

As we walked, I noticed that practically everybody said hi to Lindsay. She waved in this neat way with her hand and nodded her head. I was itching to try that wave, but was more intrigued by watching her. Sure, she was pretty, but there was something more about Lindsay that I couldn't quite put my finger on.

It was definitely more than being a TV star's daughter. I was determined to figure out what her secret was. If I could just get her and Ash together, and get Ash to fall for her and . . . you know the rest. In the meantime, I could add some valuable notes to the Guide. Even if Bev thought Lindsay was a world-class jerk, she would have to admit we had something to learn from this girl.

"So is it true that your mom is Desirée Sparks? *The* Desirée Sparks?" I asked as we neared the attendance office. I wanted to stall her—to bask in her glow for a little longer.

"Oh, yeah," she said in a bored voice.

I was amazed. "You don't sound too thrilled."

"Oh, I don't know. I mean, everybody's always making such a big deal about Mother. So what if she's a star . . . ." Lindsay's voice trailed off. "Oh, heck. She's no different than your mom."

I tried not to smile. I mean, I wouldn't trade

46

my mom for even a second, but our moms were worlds apart. Desirée Sparks was one of the most glamorous, sizzling stars in the country, a mega-celebrity. She'd been on the cover of a zillion magazines, modeling all kinds of glitzy gowns and jewels.

My mom, on the other hand, well, was attractive, but in a different, more low-key sort of way. No slinky jersey dresses with huge slits up the sides or false eyelashes for her. And she wouldn't even let *The Valley Sheet* take her picture when the Youth Club building was dedicated. She said she didn't do anything to deserve public acclaim. She was just doing her duty to the community.

"Why are you walking this way? We're heading toward the attendance office, and I sure don't want to go there." Lindsay's voice cut into my thoughts.

"I'm an office helper," I explained. "I help deliver office messages and notes from the school nurse. Stuff like that. Dull stuff," I added because a girl like Lindsay would think office work was boring.

Lindsay frowned. "Boring. I have drama class," she said. "You should try to transfer into drama. We have a good time. I love acting. It's such an escape." Her eyes looked faraway when she said that, and she made a sweep with her hand and twirled around. I nodded, and made up my mind that minute that I'd try to transfer out of the office work. Then Lindsay and I would have a class together! So what if the thought of being onstage didn't exactly appeal to me?

"What are you doing after school tomorrow?" Lindsay suddenly asked me. "Maybe I could come over to your house. Will your brother be home?"

For one minute, I felt like she'd just handed me a precious gift. But suddenly a wave of disappointment hit me as I remembered that tomorrow Ash and I were supposed to start working with the kids on the *I Love Me* program.

"Uh, well, tomorrow's not such a good day. You see, I'll be at the Youth Club. My mom is the director there, and we're doing this musical thing with some little kids."

"Ugh. What a drag," she said.

"Completely," I said, though I felt a bit disloyal to Mom just then. And then I was hit with inspiration. "You know, my brother Ash is going to be helping. He told me he wants to meet you. Why don't you come with us tomorrow? You can meet him and watch the first rehearsal for the program. Even though it's for little kids, it's kind of like drama. Then maybe some other day you could come over to my house."

"Sounds like fun," Lindsay said, with the fastest change of heart in world history. "I'll meet you tomorrow by the pay phones."

Then a horrible thought occurred to me. I'd asked Bev—and now Lindsay—to help with the *I Love Me* musical. Great. A vision came into my mind of Ash, both of his arms totally ripped off, looking at me with disgust. Bev held one arm and Lindsay held the other. And I, of course, was not too popular with anybody. I'd have to figure a way out of this mess.

As I walked to the office, I felt mixed up. On one hand, I felt incredibly happy since the Social Survival Guide was heading me for success after all. But on the other hand, I felt like a real creep for what I was about to do to Bev.

Sometime during my office errands, it hit me. If I was going to become popular, I should start trying to be more like Lindsay. I'd never look like her, of course, but I could act like her.

My mind raced ahead. I could bug my parents for some more new clothes. I'd learn to wave and smile and walk like she did. I'd call my mom "Mother." Yes, it would be good-bye to the boring old Lisa, and hello to a sparkling new Lisa! I couldn't wait to tell Bev.

But then I wondered what Bev would think of the sparkling new Lisa. Well, she wanted to be popular—at least she *used* to. I could tell her how easy it was . . . after I'd figured it out. Maybe I wouldn't tell her my new idea just yet.

After school, I went over to Bev's house.

"Toads!" shouted Bev, as I walked into her room. She was sitting upright in her bed in her flowery nightgown, surrounded by a zillion science books. Her nightgown looked at least a hundred years old. I wondered why Mrs. Davis, the housekeeper, hadn't thrown it away before this.

"What?" I asked, tossing my books onto her desk and flopping onto the white carpet.

"I've been reading about amphibians all day," Bev said, her eyes bright, and not from a fever either. "I went through all kinds of magazines and everything trying to figure out what we could do our project on. I just now got it! We can do our project on toads."

"Most normal people who are sick at home from school watch soaps and game shows on TV," I informed her. "Only a truly sick person would get all excited about a science project."

She ignored this. "Well, what do you think?"

"About toads? Well, usually I don't." I laughed. She didn't.

"Are you going to do a project with me, or aren't you?" Bev asked, sounding angry.

"Okay, okay," I said irritably, just to make her happy. Suddenly it occurred to me that maybe my Plan would work better if Bev was caught up in something like the science project. She'd be so busy, she wouldn't notice that I was helping Ash to fall madly in love with Lindsay. Well, it was worth a try. When Bev gets wrapped up in something, she's like the original absent-minded professor. "I'll be on the project with you, so don't get all bent out of shape. But only because I want to go to Disneyland. However, I will *not* do a project on toads," I thundered. Then I tried without any luck to think of a better project we could both agree upon.

And then I did something I probably shouldn't have. "Oh, by the way, Bev, Mom isn't going to need that much help with the *I Love Me* program after all. Too many helpers might distract the kids—or something. Besides, you're probably way too busy with school and the science project and stuff. I mean—I think you shouldn't have to waste your time on that silly program."

Bev just looked at me. She shrugged her shoulders and said, "Okay."

Six

BEV was absent again the next day, which was bad because I wanted her to meet Lindsay. As soon as school was over, I met Lindsay by the pay phones.

"Come on," I said. "We'll have to hurry if we're going to catch the bus to my house. Then we'll walk the block to the club."

"Do you think we can get a ride or something?" Lindsay asked. "These shoes aren't exactly the most comfortable things in the world." I looked down at her expensive, soft gray boots.

"Sorry, it's the chauffeur's day off," I said, laughing at my own joke.

Lindsay didn't smile. "It is? That's too bad."

I laughed. I guessed she took me seriously.

"Let's hurry," I said. Then I got sneaky. "Ash is probably already there by now."

At that, Lindsay's eyes brightened, and we

took off for the bus. We took seats way in the back. On the way, I shyly asked her about what it was like to be a star's kid. She stretched her legs across the aisle and put her feet on the empty seat. The bus driver watched this in the mirror, but didn't say anything. Then she started talking too loudly about her mom.

"Mother wants me to be a star, too," Lindsay said. "So I have to take dancing and singing lessons. You name it—I've taken lessons for it."

"Wow!" I breathed. I'd never taken lessons for anything in my whole life. Except a few tumbling and baton classes at the Youth Club when I was a little kid.

As soon as we got off the bus, Lindsay demanded to know where my house was.

"It's that ranch house," I pointed out as we passed it.

"It looks . . . homey," was Lindsay's only comment. I cringed inside. I knew about the humongous Tudor mansion Lindsay's family lived in. By comparison, our house looked like a mouse house.

While we walked, I watched the way Lindsay walked. It was a kind of bouncy glide. I'd simply have to practice that walk later when I was alone.

When we arrived at the Club, I could see that Mom looked hassled. There were at least twenty screaming little kids in the auditorium. They scurried underfoot and seemed to bounce off the walls. Even though there were one or two mothers helping out, I could tell Mom was happy to see us. As soon as she saw us, she smiled.

"Mom, this is Lindsay," I said introducing the two of them. I watched Mom's face to see how Lindsay registered with her. "She wants to watch and, uh, lend a hand. Bev's not coming."

If Mom caught the look Lindsay shot me just then, she didn't let on. "How good to meet you, dear," said Mom. "It's nice of you to come help. Lisa, Punkin, you're rehearsing in the supply room today. The quilting club has the auditorium."

"I totally adore kids, Mrs. Halloran," gushed Lindsay. But as soon as Mom scurried away, I noticed she plucked a little boy away from her with this really disgusted look. She hissed, "I didn't say I was going to help. I just said I'd come to watch."

"I know. You can just watch—Ash," I said soothingly, and reached down to capture the plucked kid before he darted around the corner. *How embarrassing to have to practice in a supply room,* I thought. *What will Lindsay think?*

"Where is Ash?" Lindsay asked poutily—and loudly—as we walked toward the supply room.

Suddenly we heard a crash.

"Right here," called Ash. When we opened the door, we saw Ash picking up a huge, empty glue can and calming the little boy who'd apparently knocked it down.

"Enter at your own risk," Ash said cheerfully, waving an arm at the overloaded shelves towering above him. He held out a tissue to the crying kid, who blew his nose and scampered off to join about 15 of his friends.

"Oh, gross!" muttered Lindsay. Then she kicked me hard in the shins, which I took to mean she wanted an introduction to Ash—and pronto.

"This is my friend, Lindsay," I said quickly.

"Sparks," supplied Lindsay in this cooey voice. "You've heard of Desirée Sparks, I'm sure."

Ash gave her a wave with his hand that was holding a wadded-up tissue.

"You're Desirée Sparks' daughter?" Ash asked, which was dumb because we already went over all that just the other day.

"Oh, yes," Lindsay answered, like Ash was

the smartest guy in the world. "Do you watch her show? I can't believe that's her sometimes, looking so glamorous. I mean, she's my *mother!*"

I looked down at my sneakers and studied the toes for a moment. Ash coughed. "Well, anyway, I'm glad to meet you. Thanks for helping us with the program. Get some more of your friends to help, so I can get out of this place." He paused and grinned this neat grin. Then he said, "Aw, I guess I don't really mind being here that much."

One of the mothers, Mrs. Fogarty, was in charge of the program. Now she clapped her hands to get the kids' attention. I was eager to corral the kids and get to work. I mean, I was glad Ash and Lindsay were hitting it off, but I couldn't help being a teeny bit annoyed that Lindsay didn't have to work at anything. One look at Lindsay, and Ash had turned into a blob of margarine. Maybe I was a bit jealous for Bev. She'd had her eyeballs on Ash for a whole year, and he never looked at her like that. Not even once.

"All right, first things first. Lisa, your brother suggested that you be the emcee and introduce the program. Here are your lines," Mrs. Fogarty said as she gave me a piece of paper.

Me? Onstage? I threw a panic-stricken look to Ash, but he just gave me a wicked grin. At that moment, I'd gladly have traded in my brother for any major appliance.

But Mrs. Fogarty didn't even notice the fear in my face. "Study that, Lisa, and we'll work on it next session. Okay, children," Mrs. Fogarty went on. "Here's the first song, 'I Give Myself a Hug Every Day.' It's real easy. Just watch me." Mrs. Fogarty went through the song and the hand movements. The movements consisted of self-hugs and some hand gestures. This was where we were supposed to step in. Ash and I went to work, running from kid to kid, showing them the hug stuff and keeping them in a tight group. Lindsay hummed along to the song and watched Ash.

As the hour wore on, the supply room got stuffier and stuffier. We had to stop completely every few minutes to escort a thirsty child to the drinking fountain. I began to perspire like crazy from tons of sweaty hugs from tons of sweaty kids.

"When do we get out of here?" whispered Lindsay as she walked past me toward the fountain for the zillionth time. I glared because every time she went to the fountain, all the little kids demanded a water break, too.

Then we had to gather them together to work again. Finally, Mrs. Fogarty decided to call it quits.

"Okay. That's enough for today," she yelled. "Let's all walk back to your mommies. We'll sing some more next week." I wiped my forehead, and reached down to hold some little hands.

As we walked down the hall, I noticed how Ash made a point to be right next to Lindsay. Oh, boy, my plan was beginning to work. If only I could ignore the little nudge of guilt about Bev.

Two days later, Bev called me up on the phone. It was Sunday night.

"Hey, you were supposed to call me yesterday about our science fair project," she complained.

"I'm sorry," I said. "I was buried in my history report, and I guess I forgot."

"Well, I hate to tell you this, but since we didn't have an idea of our own, Ms. Penney assigned one to us," Bev said. Then her voice got funny. "It's called 'Fun With Fungus.'"

"What!" I nearly screeched. "Where'd she come up with a dumb name like that? Well, you can forget it. Count me out!"

"You can't back out now," Bev yelled. "It's your fault we're in this mess. You wouldn't let us do toads!" she cried defensively.

"But Bev—" I protested weakly.

"A promise is a promise," Bev said. Boy, could she fight dirty when she wanted to.

"Okay," I sighed in defeat. "Fun with Fungus it is. Now how do you propose we have fun with fungus?"

"I don't know," Bev sighed. "But we have to turn in our outline tomorrow in order to enter it for the state fair on time. So start thinking and so will I. Call me after your history is finished and we'll talk some more. Maybe I can pull together some sort of outline tomorrow during study hall."

"How are we ever going to be popular if we're spending all our time having fun with fungus?" I grumbled.

Bev ignored me. "Brendan and his partner are doing their project on the effects of vodka and caffeine on goldfish," Bev added. "Isn't that a great idea?"

"Ummm," I said. With a promise to think of a fabulous fungus idea and call back later, I hung up on Bev and finished my history report.

After a while I took a candy-bar break. Then I sneaked into Ash's room. He'd gone to a friend's house to study, so I decided to do my math homework on his computer.

Entering his room was not easy. I could barely get the door open because of all the clothes scrunched behind it. "Yuck," I said, wrinkling my nose as I walked over to the computer table. However popular Ash was to the world, I alone knew a terrible secret about him—he was a slob. His room was littered with clothes, books, leftover snacks and worse. My mom had given up asking him to straighten his room. Of course, she still seemed to think I could be saved, so she bugged me daily to straighten mine.

I closed Ash's door quietly so my parents wouldn't hear me in his room. But wouldn't you know it—the minute I was seated at the computer, Bertie and Bertha scurried up to the doorway and started barking like crazy.

"Shhh," I said, getting up and opening the door to let them in. I had to quiet them quickly or Mom or Dad would come up to check out the commotion and find me in Ash's room— one place I wasn't supposed to be.

I wrestled with my math problems for a while and the dogs dozed at my feet. I tried to breathe through my mouth so I didn't have to keep catching whiffs of Eau de Sneakers or whatever it was that made Ash's room smell.

A half hour later, the problems were finished. I scratched Bertie absently behind the ears while I checked over my paper to make sure I'd done all the problems. Suddenly Bertha whined and sat upright. The hair stood up on the back of her neck as she got up and sniffed her way suspiciously over to Ash's bed.

"What is it, girl?" I asked fearfully. Maybe Bertha had discovered a mouse under Ash's bed. After all, he probably had enough half-eaten food there to feed a mouse family for a week. Bertha started yapping furiously, and Bertie joined in. I had to do something quick. Without thinking of the danger I was exposing myself to, I flipped up the bedspread and took a daring peek under the bed. The sight that greeted my eyes was far worse than a mouse colony.

There, amid several empty soda cans, a paper plate, and a number of candy wrappers was an old, plastic microwave plate. And it was growing hair—gross, furry, fuchsia-colored hair. Bertie seemed to jump back in horror, while Bertha continued to sniff frantically. Then they both started to bark again. I plugged my nose, then gingerly carried the offensive plate down to the kitchen.

"It's okay," I said, trying to soothe the dogs as I breathed through my mouth. They must not have believed me because they kept on barking.

"What's going on?" my dad called from the family room where he was watching TV.

"Nothing," I called back while holding the plate as far away from me as possible. I set the disgusting mess in the sink. It would have to wait until someone could load it into the dishwasher tomorrow. That someone would not be me if I could help it. I slipped out of the kitchen and didn't give my disgusting discovery another thought. It was time to lose myself in the pages of *The Mystery of the Twisted Tiara*.

Minutes later, the phone rang. I pulled myself reluctantly away from my book to answer it. *Bev and the project,* I groaned to myself as I picked up the receiver. But it was Lindsay.

"Hi," she said. "What are you doing?"

"Uh, reading," I answered, then instantly decided that was the wrong thing to say. I didn't want Lindsay to think I was boring. "Reading through my brother's high-school yearbook. What are you doing?"

"Oh, nothing much. Just finished dinner with Mother and some of her weird entertainment friends. The whole thing was a big yawn," Lindsay said.

I conjured up a swirly image of movie stars and Hollywood types gathered around a glittery table, talking and laughing. It sounded so exciting. How could Lindsay be so bored with it all?

"Listen," she said. "I just wanted to know if Ash has said anything about me in the last couple of days?"

That threw me off guard. I mean, Ash isn't the kind to talk about girls—well, at least not to me.

"Well, no," I said, twisting the phone cord.

"Oh, so he doesn't like me?" Lindsay said, her voice suddenly crystal cool. "Hang on a minute." Then I heard her say something like, "Sheila, please set my school clothes out for tomorrow."

I realized I'd made a big mistake. I'd better let Lindsay know our friendship was paying off, or I had the uncomfortable feeling she'd drop me just like that.

"Well, I'll have to get you together with him some more," I babbled. "I mean, it's obvious he was interested in you. It's just . . . well, Ash doesn't rush into things."

I felt like Ash's personal girlfriend broker just then. But I guessed I'd said the right thing because Lindsay was nicer after that.

"Well, come join my friends and me on the front lawn tomorrow. We'll talk some more," she said before she hung up.

I set the phone in the cradle and hugged myself. Lindsay had invited me to hang out with her group! I slid into bed a few minutes later, hardly daring to believe it. What a great start—just what the Guide was meant to give me! Now, if only I could figure out a way for Bev to share my good luck.

The next morning after I dressed, I went downstairs to the kitchen. I flipped on the light and looked in the sink. The fuchsia-colored stuff was still growing in a mound on the microwave plate.

All of a sudden, in a rush, I remembered that I was supposed to call Bev last night about our "Fun with Fungus" project. I looked back at the sink. "Aha!" I crowed. If it was fungus Bev wanted, then fungus she would have. Fuchsia fungus. I picked up the horrible plate out of the sink, rushed outside and hid it out back in the toolshed where it wouldn't be disturbed.

Later that morning, when Bev came over so we could walk to the bus stop, I grabbed her arm. "Come on," I said quickly. "I have to show you something in the toolshed."

"Why do you have such a mysterious look on your face?" Bev asked as she followed me.

"Shhh," I said, putting my finger to my lips. I flung back the door.

"What—" began Bev. "What is that?"

"That," I said triumphantly, "is fungus. *That* is our science project."

"Gross!" she exclaimed.

"Ms. Penney won't think so," I replied.

Bev's face lit up as she realized I was right. She chattered excitedly all the way to school about my fungal find. She must have asked me a zillion times how I found it. I felt pretty lucky just then. I'd found our project without even trying.

As soon as we arrived at school, I spotted Lindsay chatting with a group of kids on the front lawn. I glanced at Bev, unsure about how I was going to break away from her to go up to Lindsay's group. The minute Lindsay saw me, she waved and motioned me over. She was wearing this animal-print shirt with black pants and lots of gold jewelry. Unwillingly, my eyes slid down Bev and me, the two Miss Blahs of Foothill Middle.

"Hi," Lindsay said breathlessly. I prayed she wouldn't say a word about Ash and the *I Love Me* program in front of Bev.

"Bev, this is Lindsay," I said quickly. "And this is my friend, Bev."

Lindsay narrowed her eyes and checked Bev over slowly with a kind of mean look. I glanced quickly at Bev. I could see that she didn't like that look one little bit.

"Nice to meet you," Bev said in a tight voice. "Listen, Lisa, I'm running up to the library to work on the outline. Coming?"

I shook my head and sucked in my breath, hoping Bev wouldn't be too mad. She just gave me a weird look and took off quickly down the walkway.

"When can you get Ash and me together again?" Lindsay asked. Wow, she worked quickly. I blinked.

"Uh, well, just come to a couple more rehearsals, then I'm sure I can work something else out," I said. I sure couldn't think of anything else just then.

"Well, all right. Come on over and join the others," Lindsay said. I glanced at her crowd. It consisted of Maria and Lori, among others. Lindsay saw the way I hung back.

"Oh, come on," she said airily. "They know you're my friend—now."

The way she said that made me uneasy. But wasn't this what I'd been hoping for ever since the Social Survival Guide and Lindsay came together in my mind? I smiled bravely and said, "Sure. Why not?"

You should have seen the look Lori and Maria gave me as we walked up to them. At first they kind of ignored me. But Lindsay kept including me in the conversation, and before long they said a few things to me, too. By the time the bell rang. I could really feel the change in the way they all treated me. The Social Survival Guide was working. I, Lisa Halloran, was on the way to being accepted by the popular people!

Seven

YOU'D think that once I was noticed by the popular kids at school everything would be easy. But let me tell you, it was work. There were lots of unspoken rules to this business of being popular. Our Social Survival Guide hadn't even begun to find them all. I had finally managed to stop taking notes about popularity—and was living it!

The next few days at school seemed like a dream come true. Lori and Maria and their friends stopped to talk to me in the halls. I ate on the popular patch of lawn at lunch. My phone rang at home, but not just with calls for Ash. Some were for me! A week later, I was invited to two slumber parties for the weekend after next—and on the same night! People who'd never talked to me before now smiled and waved at me in the halls.

The only thing that messed it up was that

Bev kept making excuses not to sit with us at lunch. She always seemed to disappear whenever Lindsay and her friends were around. Dumb, huh? I mean, here was our chance to be popular together, and she was blowing it.

I decided it was time for a serious friend-to-friend talk. One Saturday afternoon, I hooked Bertie and Bertha on their leashes and took them over to Bev's house with me. I knocked loudly.

Mrs. Davis, the Hansen's housekeeper, answered the door.

"Oh, it's you, Lisa. Bev will be right down." Then she gave me a look that said "No Dogs Allowed." As if I didn't know better.

A minute later, Bev appeared at the door. "Hi," she said, looking down at her feet. I suddenly felt kind of uncomfortable with her, too. It was weird how suddenly best friends could be shy with each other. "What's going on?"

"Nothing," I said. "Want to come on a walk with me? We can stop and get some ice cream if you want."

"Sure," she said. We started down the street, neither of us talking. Bev kept twiddling the friendship bracelet I'd made her. I kept trying to think of things to say, but didn't know where to start.

"Why are you starting to ignore me at school?" she blurted out.

"*Me* ignore *you*?" I said hotly. "You're the one who ignores me whenever I'm with Lindsay and the others. Why? Do you hate them?"

"No, of course not. I don't even know them. Now don't get all mad," Bev said. "It's just—just that you're suddenly spending so much time with them."

"Why shouldn't I?" I demanded. I didn't mean to be mean. Really I didn't, but Bev made me mad. Me ignoring her?

"No reason. But I guess I just don't like hanging around that group."

"Well, you might if you'd only try to get to know them," I reasoned.

"Yeah."

"Well, let's not fight," I finally said. "We're still best friends, right?"

Bev nodded.

"It's just that I thought we both wanted to be popular. Wasn't that why we both worked so hard on the Social Survival Guide?"

Bev shrugged. "I guess I don't want to be popular that badly after all."

"What do you mean?" I asked.

"Look, Lisa. I guess I just realized that having lots of friends is one thing. You don't have

70

to do complete personality makeovers to have friends. That particular group of kids you hang out with, well, they're popular all right. But they do things in a way that feels weird to me. Oh, I don't know. It just seems to me you've changed a lot over these last few weeks," Bev said.

"I haven't changed. You have!" I declared. We stood facing each other in the street, neither of us giving the other an inch. Bertha and Bertie started jumping all over us. I pushed the dogs off, suddenly feeling tired.

"You know, all of a sudden I'm not that hungry for ice cream," Bev said. "I think I'll go home."

"Fine," I snapped, then turned down the street to continue my walk—alone. The more I walked, the madder I got. And since I walked a lot, I got pretty mad.

I was so busy thinking about how weird Bev was being that I didn't notice a huge orange cat that darted across the street. Bertie and Bertha did, though. They jerked on their leashes and started yapping wildly, jerking me right out of my thoughts. The cat shot down the street, and so did Bertie, Bertha, and I. It took forever to get the dogs under control again. Then I realized we had walked for blocks, all the way to Crescent Street, in fact. Just down the street was the giant Tudor house where Lindsay lived. *Well, good,* I thought. *I'll go visit her.*

"Come on, you bad dogs," I said to Bertie and Bertha, giving their leashes a shake. The little dogs gave me a sheepish look, and we continued up the street.

As we walked, it occurred to me that I'd better work on getting Ash and Lindsay together again. Trouble was, I couldn't think of how to do that outside of the *I Love Me* rehearsals. Ash was always so busy after school with his gymnastics practice and all his friends. I sighed. Like it or not, Lindsay would have to be happy with seeing Ash at the Youth Club until I could think of something better.

I stopped in front of Lindsay's house and drew in my breath sharply. I'd never realized just how huge it was before. The lawn seemed to go on for acres, and the house looked like an English castle. I stared up at the leaded windows of the second story and wondered which room was Lindsay's. Funny thing, she never invited me or any of the kids over to her house. I knew this because several of my new friends asked me if I'd met the famous Desirée Sparks yet. Apparently, none of them had met her either.

Bertie and Bertha went crazy again at the

sound of a motor that came from behind the house, and I yanked on their leashes. A long, fancy gray car came gliding down the driveway. The man driving it was wearing a cap and a uniform. *So Lindsay's family has a chauffeur,* I thought to myself. I watched as the car glided down the street.

"Shoo, you crazy little dogs. Get away from here," came a sharp voice right behind me. I nearly jumped out of my skin. Turning around, I could see that the voice belonged to a plump woman wearing a gray uniform with a white lace collar.

"I'm . . . uh . . . a friend of Lindsay's. Is she here? Could I see her?" I stammered. People in uniforms made me nervous. I wondered if that woman was the same Sheila who laid out Lindsay's school clothes for her.

She looked me over. I guess she decided I wasn't a kidnapper or anything.

"Come through the gate," the maid said. She led the way up the drive to a side door. I waited on the step while the maid disappeared inside. After a minute Lindsay opened the door a crack. I noticed her hair was a mess and her face was blotchy. She'd been crying.

"Hi," she said, her voice wavering. "What are you doing here?"

"I . . . I just stopped by. I was walking my

dogs," I said, waiting for her to invite me in. I wondered if I should ask why she was crying.

"Well, you'd better not let my dogs see yours. They're Great Danes. They'll gulp yours down in a single bite."

"Oh," I said, and pulled Bertha and Bertie closer to me. Lindsay made no move to invite me in.

"Uh, I just wanted to remind you about the rehearsal for the *I Love Me* program after school on Monday. Can you come?" I asked, quickly thinking of an excuse for coming over.

"Yeah, tell Ash I'll be there," Lindsay said. She started to close the door.

I decided I'd definitely caught Lindsay at a bad time. "I, uh, had better go," I stammered.

"I'll buzz the gate open for you," Lindsay called. We waved good-bye, and I puzzled about her strange behavior for a while. The rest of the way home, I wondered what Lindsay had to cry about.

*   *   *   *   *

Monday morning, Bev and I walked to school together as usual, but what wasn't so usual was that we didn't talk much. There just didn't seem to be much to say. Oh, of course, we talked about the fungus project for a bit.

Bev wanted to move the microwave plate and its furry resident over to her house where it wouldn't be disturbed.

"I'm afraid something will happen to it at your house," she explained.

"Oh," I said, without interest.

As soon as we got to school, Bev waved good-bye the minute we spotted Lindsay and the crowd. I glared at her retreating back, then sighed. *Fine,* I thought. *If she wants to be that way, who cares.* I walked off to join my new friends.

"What are you wearing to Lori's slumber party?" asked Regina Hayes, a pretty short-haired girl who giggled more than she talked. She was twisting a strand of her long hair around her finger and looking at me intently.

I was just about to tell her about a peach sweater set I was considering when Lindsay interrupted. "You guys haven't asked me what I'm going to wear," she said casually.

Instantly about ten pairs of eyes were glued on Lindsay. She didn't say anything for a minute, but all eyes remained fixed on her.

"Well, tell us, Lindsay," wheedled Maria finally. "What is it?"

"You really want to know?" Lindsay said with a teasing note. "I guess I'd better wait and let it be a surprise." Then she tossed back her hair. And though the other girls begged and begged, she wouldn't breathe another word. Finally the bell rang for first period, and the group split apart to go to class. Lindsay motioned with her head for me to follow her to her locker.

"I can't. I'll be late," I said because her locker was the opposite way to my class. But I trotted alongside her through the crowd in the hallway anyway.

"Listen, Lisa," Lindsay said, not even looking at me. "I'm going to need your help today."

Oh, that was different. "Oh, yeah?" I asked. "With what?"

"I need to get out of drama class. You have office work third period. Bring a note to my class that says the school nurse needs to see me. Okay?" Lindsay stopped by her locker and looked right into my eyes.

I looked down. "Uh, it's not that easy," I mumbled.

"What did you say?" she said, with those eyes again.

I gulped. That icy stare reminded me of some not-so-hot days when I sat and wondered what it felt like to hang out where the cool kids hung out.

"I just said it wasn't that easy, but I'll figure something out," I assured her.

Instantly Lindsay's face brightened. She placed her hand on my shoulder.

"Thanks. I knew I could count on you. You're a real friend," she said.

She turned to her locker, and I ducked down the hallway, breaking into a sprint so I'd make it to class on time.

You're a real friend. I repeated the words to myself a zillion times that morning before third period. The words filled me with a warm glow. I mean, here was Lindsay, a TV star's daughter—a pretty, popular girl who could have anyone at Foothill for her friend. And she chose me, so I'd better not let her down.

When third period rolled around, I reported to the office. As usual, there was a stack of messages I was supposed to take around to teachers in their classrooms. When no one was looking, I grabbed an extra class excuse slip off the school secretary's desk and filled it out with Lindsay's name and the time.

"I'm off," I said, and waved to Mrs. Simpson.

I flew down the hallways and gave out the messages, saving Lindsay's for last. I tried not to think about what I was about to do. I'd never done anything like this before, and I was one of the few student office workers Mrs. Simpson trusted to carry messages. *You're a real friend.* The words echoed in my ears again.

I spotted Lindsay immediately when I walked into the drama class. A few students were seated in groups in the auditorium, reading lines from script books. Lindsay was onstage with a single spotlight trained on her. Under the bright lights, I could see her face was flushed, and she was arguing loudly with a boy and Mr. Mosely, the teacher.

"Kevin's saying his lines all wrong!" Lindsay was shouting. "Don't you think I should know what I'm talking about?"

Mr. Mosely was gesturing wildly and trying to say something. I cleared my throat and walked up to the stage. When Lindsay saw me, she dropped her angry face and flashed me a quick smile.

I walked past her and gave the fake message to Mr. Mosely.

He looked at Lindsay for a moment, then sighed. "You're wanted in the nurse's office. We'll work this out later. You may sit down, now, Kevin. Next group, please," he said, sounding tired.

I walked off the stage quickly, so it didn't look suspicious. A few seconds later, I heard Lindsay's footsteps behind me.

"Thanks," she breathed in my ear.

"You all looked pretty mad. What was going on in there?" I asked.

"Nothing. Just another screaming match. Thank heavens you got me out of that class. We were working on these stupid scenes, and that stupid teacher doesn't realize Kevin's just hopeless. I shouldn't have to be stuck with him," Lindsay blurted out. "My mother won't let me transfer out either. So I'm just going to cut every chance I can."

"Oh," I said, getting more bewildered by the minute. Just a couple of weeks ago, Lindsay had told me how much fun drama class was. I sure didn't understand her.

"Let's go upstairs," Lindsay said. I followed her. At the top of the stairs, she leaned over the balcony. I leaned over with her.

Below us, we watched Joe, the janitor, blowing dirt off the walkway with a noisy blowing machine. I looked down at Lindsay's shoes. They were cute and made of dark red leather with a couple of straps crisscrossing over them.

"I like your shoes," I said.

"I hate them," Lindsay said suddenly.

Her tone made me look up at her in surprise. I watched in horror as she kicked them off over the balcony. One of the shoes landed in the ivy. Lindsay laughed wildly when she

79

saw Joe pick it up and look around.

"Let's get out of here!" she hissed, grabbing me away from the balcony.

I ran alongside her down the hall, puzzled and shaking my head. Why would Lindsay do a thing like that?

"Won't your mother kill you?" I asked her breathlessly while we skipped down the stairs. I knew for a fact my mom would skin me alive for throwing away a perfectly good pair of shoes.

"Are you kidding?" Lindsay laughed gleefully, in a way that made me uneasy. She danced along the hallway in her stocking feet. "She'll probably have already bought me three new pairs by the time I get home. She won't even notice those stupid ones are missing!"

I laughed, but I wasn't quite sure why I was laughing.

"Well, I guess I'd better get back to the office," I mumbled uncomfortably.

"Fine. By the way, when do I get to see Ash again?" Lindsay asked.

"I told you . . . today after school," I said to her.

Lindsay rolled her eyes. "I don't love *I Love Me*," she said, then giggled. "But it's all for a good cause, I guess."

"See you," I said, then started back for the

office, hoping I hadn't been gone too long.

I wondered about Lindsay and the shoes she threw over the balcony. I also wondered what she did without shoes. But since she was nowhere to be found during lunch, I decided that she must have skipped out on school for the rest of the day. So I guessed she wouldn't be waiting for me by the pay phones after school.

I was wrong. She was there waiting. And she'd changed her clothes. She was now wearing a cute royal blue sweatshirt with a big gray dolphin appliquéd on it. She had on a royal blue knit skirt to match.

"Oh, there you are," she said. "Come on, William is waiting for us."

I was mystified. "Who's William?" I asked.

"Our driver," she said. "Hurry up."

I almost broke into a run to keep up with Lindsay as she walked briskly toward the parking lot. Right behind the school bus, I saw the long, gray car I'd seen slither down Lindsay's driveway the other day.

"But, Lindsay," I sputtered. "The Youth Club is o—"

Lindsay cut in. "Only a block from your house. I know. But I don't want to take that rickety old bus again. And I sure don't want to walk." That tone again.

William opened the back door for us and we slid in. I sat on the edge of the seat, unsure of how to sit in a car like this. Lindsay took one look at me and laughed.

"It's just like any other car!" she said, and laughed a tinkly laugh.

"Right," I said. I watched the kids watching us with open mouths as we pulled away from the curb. Lindsay waved gaily at some of the kids we ate lunch with. I waved, too. It was pretty neat riding in a limousine. I sank back into the soft leather seats and leaned down to feel the plush, velvety gray carpet.

"I like to do stuff like this every once in a while to shake people up," Lindsay said to me as she rolled up her window. Then she cranked up the radio and drummed her fingers to the music.

"What's this?" I asked, pointing to a silver holder by my door.

"That's for flowers," Lindsay explained matter-of-factly.

"Oh," I said. Rich people put flowers in their cars?

"Hey, you want to call someone?" Lindsay asked, picking up the car phone.

"Uh, no thanks," I said. I'd liked to have called Bev, but that wouldn't do.

"Did you notice my new shoes?" Lindsay

asked. "What did I tell you? Three new pairs were waiting for me at home."

Mom was standing out on the sidewalk talking to Mrs. Fogarty when we pulled up in front of the Youth Club. She looked at me with a steady gaze as William assisted me and Lindsay out. I gave her an uneasy wave. It made me feel real funny to be climbing out of a limousine in front of my mom.

"Uh, hi, Mom," I called.

Lindsay walked over to join us. "Hi, Mrs. Halloran. We're here to help out again," she said cheerily as if she couldn't wait one more minute to be with those little kids.

"It's nice to see you again, dear," Mom said in her most momlike voice, but I noticed her giving Lindsay this steady, questioning look. "Ash and Ryan are already in the supply room. Run along. Mrs. Fogarty will be right there."

"Just in time," Ash said as we walked in. "Freddy spilled some poster paint. Grab some rags and help mop up."

"Oh, not me," Lindsay piped up. "Don't you have a janitor or something to clean it up?"

Ryan shot Lindsay a look.

"Oh, no," I quickly agreed with Lindsay. "You'll ruin your cute shirt. You just sit there, and I'll clean it up."

Somehow Ryan, Ash, and I managed to clean the mess and have the children seated on the floor in a circle by the time my mom and Mrs. Fogarty came into the room.

Mrs. Fogarty clapped her hands and said cheerily, "Okay, kids, let's show Mrs. Halloran how we give ourselves a hug every day!"

Lindsay rolled her eyes at me. I pretended not to see and started helping the kids with their hugs. My mom left after the first song, and we started to work on the other songs. One was called, "I Feel Good About Me." It had some funny little dancelike steps to it.

The kids did better with this one, surprisingly enough, though it was harder than the hug song. Lindsay sat in the back of the room while the rest of us hopped and skipped to the song.

There was no mistaking the look Ash gave me a few minutes into this routine. He was plainly saying, "What's that Lindsay girl doing here?" I stuck my tongue out at him on general principles. Then Mrs. Fogarty left the room to make a phone call.

Lindsay took the opportunity to say in her sweetest voice to Ash, "Would you please get me something diet to drink? I'm dying of thirst."

Well, that did it. Immediately two dozen

grubby little kids demanded soft drinks, too, and any hope we had of getting through the "I Feel Good About Me" song was shattered. During the confusion that followed, one kid managed to bop another on the head with a paint stirrer.

"Owww!" he cried loudly.

Ash glared at me. I tried to calm the bopped kid while Ash collared the wrongdoer. I felt an icy nervousness come over me. I mean, what if Ash hated Lindsay forever because of this?

Just then, wouldn't you know it, my mom walked in to witness the complete chaos. She shot me an I'm-very-disappointed-in-you look as if it were my fault.

"I don't believe there's any point in continuing for today," she said soothingly to the kids. "Let's go back to the arts and crafts room until your mommies come for you, kids."

She and the boys helped herd the kids up the hall while I looked unhappily at Lindsay.

"Well, don't look at me like that," she snapped. "All I did was ask for something to drink." She crossed her arms across her chest. "I'm calling William for a ride home. See you tomorrow." With a flounce, she walked out of the supply room, leaving one very miserable me.

I was sitting down on a stack of flattened

boxes, feeling sorry for myself, when Ash walked back into the room.

"Where's Miss Snob?" he asked.

"Gone," I said miserably.

"Why do you hang around that girl so much?" Ash asked. Then, after a minute, he asked, "Where's Bev been these days?"

"I thought you couldn't stand Bev," I shot back.

Ash leaned up against the wall, his thumbs hooked in the belt loops of his tattered jeans.

"I never said that," he said slowly. "But I definitely prefer her to Lindsay. What do you see in her anyway? Besides the fact that she's a TV star's daughter."

"Hey, that's not fair." I jumped quickly on that one. "Her mom has nothing to do with anything. Lindsay would be popular no matter who her mom was."

Ash gave a low whistle. "Oh, so that's it," he said. "You're hoping some of her popularity will rub off on you. I've got—"

"Shut up—" I began, but Ash went on.

"—news for you. There's popularity and there's popularity. She's got the wrong kind."

I was mystified. There were wrong kinds of popularity? That had never crossed my mind before. But then, what did Ash know? He was just a . . . a guy.

"Oh, yeah? What do you know? Just because you consider yourself Mr. Popularity doesn't mean you know everything about it."

Ash looked sad. "No," he said softly. "But I've learned one or two things. Being popular costs. And some people pay more than others."

"Huh?"

"Oh, never mind." Ash suddenly straightened up and unhooked his thumbs. "Come on. I'll take you home. It's my turn to cook dinner. Then we've got to figure out how to get this program together by next week or Mom's budget will be a goner for sure."

I rode home in silence, ignoring Ryan and Ash's clowning around in the front seat. I was thinking about what I was going to wear to one of the upcoming slumber parties—and trying not to think about what my know-it-all brother had said!

Eight

A few days later, I'd practically forgotten about my conversation with Ash. Plus, it seemed Lindsay had completely forgotten about the rehearsal disaster. She didn't say a word about it—or about Ash either. I was glad because I still hadn't figured out how I was going to get Ash to forget what Lindsay had done. And I knew I'd better think of something or I could kiss both my new friends *and* my newfound popularity good-bye.

Things continued to get worse with me and Bev. I mean, we weren't actually fighting or anything, but we just didn't seem to have much to say to each other. She had kind of drifted to eating lunch with a new group of kids. We were still working on the science project together, but Bev was doing most of the work. After all, the fungus was now at her house in her dad's office. She recorded its growth daily on a chart she had made.

"You know, it doesn't seem to be growing as fast lately," she said one day. "I asked my dad about it, and he told me to change its environment a little and see if that affects its growth pattern any.

"I moved the fungus on its plate where it can get some more light," Bev told me. "Fungi are plants, and plants need sunlight. But nothing seems to have changed."

I kept tabs on the fungal findings through Bev, but I didn't go to more than one or two science club meetings. For one thing, I seemed to be incredibly busy. Lindsay wanted me to go around with her everywhere. And as long as I kind of kept on top of what was happening with our project, I figured it didn't matter.

One day just as lunch period was ending, Bev walked by the patch of lawn where Lindsay and I were sitting.

"Hey, Lisa," she said without looking at Lindsay. "Too bad you missed the meeting just now. We showed our preliminary notes to Ms. Penney. She's real interested in our project and wants to come over this afternoon to meet Charlie."

"Who's Charlie?" asked Lindsay, inspecting her brightly polished fingernails.

"Yeah, who's Charlie?" I echoed.

"Charlie, our fungus. He needed a name. That's what I named him," Bev explained. "So can you come over to my house after school?"

"No. Lisa's coming to my house this afternoon," Lindsay said swiftly before I had a chance to answer.

"Uh, yeah," I stammered, though that was the first I'd heard of this plan. But actually, I was dying to see Lindsay's room, so I wouldn't have missed it for the world. "That's right, I am."

"Fine," Bev said angrily, her green eyes flashing. "I just thought you'd like to be there. After all, it's your project too, in case you've forgotten." Then she stalked off.

I felt my eyes sting, but I didn't have a chance to think about what just happened. Immediately the other kids gathered around me. "Oh, who needs her?" said Lori.

"That's right," chimed in Maria. "Those kids in the science club aren't our type anyway."

The bell rang, and we all gathered up our books to go to class. Lindsay, as usual, didn't have any books. "Oh, smile," she said, falling into step beside me. "What do you care about some stupid old gross fungus? Anyway, if you ask me, it's kind of weird to give it a name."

I didn't find it weird at all. I mean, it was a

living thing. People named their pets all the time. But I didn't say anything.

"Why don't you just tell Bev you don't want to be on the project anymore," Lindsay suggested. She laughed lightly. "After all, you have better things to do now."

I shrugged and considered it. That sure wasn't a bad idea. I had wished again and again I had never agreed to be on the project.

"You're right," I said.

"Meet me by the pay phones after school," Lindsay called as she turned to walk to her class.

I walked to class thinking of how much better it would be to be freed of the stupid project. And I was cheered up that finally I was being invited over to Lindsay's house. The other kids would really be impressed when they found out.

It seemed like forever until school ended that day. Lindsay met me by the pay phones, and we walked over to the parking lot. This time, I didn't even flinch when I saw the gray limousine. I nodded to William as I'd seen Lindsay do when we climbed in. On the way to Lindsay's house, we played with the stereo. Then Lindsay closed a sliding window that separated the driver's compartment from the passenger area. She shouted a few words just to show me that William couldn't hear a thing we said.

* * * * *

Lindsay's room was incredible. It was decorated with pretty floral wallpaper and white wicker furniture. She had her own TV and stereo and even her own bathroom. But best of all, she must have had at least a hundred books.

"Wow!" I breathed, fingering some of my favorite titles lovingly. "Have you read them all?"

Lindsay shrugged. "Some of them. My parents gave them to me, but I hate reading."

"How can you?" I asked incredulously.

Lindsay didn't answer. She opened her window that overlooked the courtyard. I leaned out for a look.

"Wow!" I gasped. "What a gorgeous pool! And what are those? Stables?"

"Yeah," Lindsay said. "Old Mr. Lindstrom, the guy who used to live here, used to keep some horses. Now we use it for the gardening stuff."

I turned around and sat down on the floral comforter on Lindsay's bed. I'd never seen such a pretty bedroom in my life. I wanted to memorize every detail.

"I hate this house," said Lindsay suddenly.

"What?"

"You heard me," Lindsay said. "I hate it. It's a total fake. Just like Mother and Father. Just like everything about our lives."

I couldn't believe what I was hearing. I just sat there.

"You want to know why Mother isn't here right now to meet my new friend?" she demanded. Her eyes were flashing and her cheeks were turning bright red.

"Uh, she's at work?" I ventured.

"Right."

"Well, lots of people's mothers work. My mom works. What's the big deal?" I asked.

"Yeah, well even when Mother isn't at work, she's at work," Lindsay shouted. Then she picked up a tennis racket that was leaning against the wall and smacked it through the air.

"Oh, forget it. You don't want to hear my silly problems," she said bitterly.

"I don't mind," I said softly.

Lindsay seemed to look right through me, but she didn't say any more. Then we went downstairs and fixed ourselves a snack in the huge kitchen and watched videos in a room that was set up like a miniature auditorium. Lindsay didn't say another word about her mother for the rest of the afternoon.

I didn't get around to calling Bev about the project that day, or the next few days. I was just too busy. First it was with another *I Love Me* rehearsal that, thank goodness, went okay. Ash was pretty nice to Lindsay, and she didn't do anything to throw the rehearsal off track.

Then by the end of the week, I could think of nothing else except Lori's slumber party. I thought guiltily about Bev while Lindsay and the gang and I sat around eating cheese popcorn. We were gossiping and telling silly stories until Lori's parents called, "Lights out!" Not too much different from the parties Bev and I used to go to.

When I got home late Saturday morning, I noticed the yards and yards of toilet paper draped from the huge old pine trees in our yard.

"Your girlfriends again," I said to Ash, giggling when we met up in the kitchen. "What was that you were telling me the other day about how popularity wasn't all that it was cracked up to be?" I teased.

Ash merely reddened. "Aw, those goofy cheerleaders probably TP'd the whole team. We won our gymnastics meet against Hart High last night. We're in the state championships for sure," he said as he gulped down the whole carton of milk. Bertha and Bertie sat at his feet, wondering if any spills would materialize.

Just then, my mom walked into the kitchen. "After you shower, Lisa, get dressed in comfy clothes. You and I are going downtown to hit the month-end sales," she said, striking dread in my heart.

I hate it when my mom drags me out shopping. No, I don't mean the kind of shopping where I go with friends to the mall and buy something with my baby-sitting money. I mean the kind where my mother takes me to the budget basement of one of those huge department stores and insists I try on every outfit my size that's on sale.

"But it looks perfect on you," she always says when I protest and tell her I will not be caught dead in such an outfit.

And this time, although I pleaded with her, Mom wouldn't take no for an answer. A few hours later, we'd hit at least three department stores. I was carrying a large shopping bag, and my mom was carrying at least three. You should have seen her. She was so happy. Bargains make her day.

But I was pretty cranky. For one thing I was tired of the crowds of shoppers. And another, I was steaming because Mom wouldn't let me buy a pair of gray boots I'd seen that looked like Lindsay's. She said they were too expensive. Finally around one o'clock, we stopped for lunch at a department store restaurant.

"I think it's so nice when you and I get a chance to do something together like this," Mom said. "I feel bad sometimes. I'm so busy all the time, and you're growing up so fast. Imagine. You're in eighth grade already."

I didn't see what there was to imagine. Eighth grade was all too real to me, so I didn't say anything. I played with the paper that came on my straw and wondered what Lindsay was doing today. Probably shopping with her mom on Rodeo Drive.

"Look, Punkin," my mom gushed over the menu. "Today's special is cream of celery soup. You always like that."

I grunted and spun around on one of the counter stools. "Mom," I burst out in exasperation, "why don't we ever go shop at fun places?"

"Hmmm?" She was busy scanning the menu.

"I mean, why don't we shop on Rodeo Drive?" I persisted.

My mom set her menu down and gave me The Look.

"There are lots of reasons we don't shop on

Rodeo Drive," she said slowly. "But I guess the main reason we don't shop on Rodeo Drive is the stores there don't sell anything we can afford to buy."

Just then the waitress came up and asked Mom what we wanted to order. And after she left, Mom turned back to me. She ruffled the top of my head with her hand and sighed.

"Well, Lindsay shops there, and her clothes are always cute," I said, trying to get her to see my point. I was thinking about the pair of gray boots I'd wanted but Mom had said I didn't need. I thought about Lindsay's mom buying her the three pairs of shoes that one afternoon. And Lindsay hadn't even asked for them.

Mom stirred her coffee and gave me a serious smile. "Lindsay's clothes may be more expensive, but you're loved," she said firmly. "Count your blessings."

I was about to ask her how she knew Lindsay wasn't loved, but I didn't. Instead I waited for my lunch and played with my straw some more.

Later that afternoon, we pulled up the driveway to our house. Just as I got out of the car, I heard the phone ring. I ran to get it, only to find it was Bev.

"Hi, Lisa. You've got to come over right

away. I've been calling you all afternoon!" she said, obviously upset.

Something must be very wrong. I gripped the phone tightly. "Why? What's the matter?"

"It's Charlie the fungus! Something's wrong with him."

I sighed. Unbelievable. I'd thought it was something serious.

"Why? What's it doing?" I asked. I wasn't about to call *it* a *him*.

"That's just it. He's not doing anything. He's still not growing. And I care about this project—even if you don't," Bev burst out.

Something explosive went off inside me right then. I mean, the whole thing was driving me insane. I had a lot of things to think about these days. Fungus wasn't one of them.

"Bev," I said slowly, "I'm sorry, but I guess you're right. I just don't care about fungus or the project. I mean, I feel bad that you're having to do the whole thing by yourself anyway. I think you might as well get all the glory. I've decided I want off the project."

"Great. Have it your way," Bev snapped. "Although I know *you* didn't decide. Lindsay and your new friends probably decided for you that you should bail out of your responsibilities!"

I was getting mad. "Wait a minute, Don't

say 'your friends' like that. They could have been your friends too—if you hadn't bailed out of *your* responsibility. We were supposed to get popular *together* . . . remember?"

Bev didn't say anything for a long moment, and I began to wonder if she'd hung up. Finally she said in a low voice, "Funny, when you think about it, we didn't plan a Social Survival Guide at all. I guess we ended up with a Social Wrecker Guide. Good-bye, Lisa."

Then she did hang up. And so did I. I was almost in tears when Ash and Ryan came into the family room a while later. They turned on the TV loud enough to send Bertha and Bertie running for cover under the sofa. Then they sprawled out on the floor reading a stack of *Gymnastics Now!* magazines that they'd dragged in.

"What are you looking so cheerful about?" Ash asked.

I glanced at Ash and Ryan, not sure whether or not I should tell them that I had probably just lost my best friend. But I was feeling so bad, I had to tell someone.

"Oh, I dropped out of the science project, and Bev's mad at me," I said.

Ash flipped through his magazine without even looking up. "Aww, she'll get over it soon enough."

"I really don't think so," I said. "She hates Lindsay and my new friends. All of them."

"All of them? I didn't know you had so many," Ryan teased.

"So it sounds like the little lady's got the popularity blues," said Ash in this twangy voice. Immediately, Bertha and Bertie scrambled out from under the sofa and started barking.

I put my hands over my ears and shouted, "Stop it!"

When the din died down, Ash said in a more serious voice, "You know, I'm serious. People always want to be popular. They think that popular people have it all. They don't see the hard part—the things people have to give up to be part of the crowd. Like friends."

I sat up, hugging my knees. "Oh, give me a break," I muttered. "You've always made tons of friends right off the bat. It's all been so easy for you."

"You think so?" Ash said, standing up and jamming his fists into his pockets. Then he walked over to the brick fireplace and stood with his back to me. "You think it's easy being 'on' all the time? When you feel you have to smile and agree with everybody all the time because they expect you to be Mr. Nice Guy?

"I look at you and see what you're giving up

to make this Lindsay girl and her goofy friends like you. It just makes me mad, that's all. I liked you better when you were just trying to be you—not a carbon copy of some spoiled rich girl."

I jumped up and felt my face grow hot. "That's a rotten thing to say," I yelled and ran from the room.

The trouble was, I knew Ash was right on this one.

Nine

LINDSAY and I headed over to the bus the following Monday.

"Mother needs the car today," Lindsay said.

I was glad. I was beginning to think I could do without the limousine. Today Lindsay wanted to sit in the front of the bus right behind the bus driver. She sang so loudly along with the radio that the bus driver finally asked her to stop.

"What a grouch," grumbled Lindsay.

"Is anything wrong Lindsay?" I whispered to her. She'd seemed tense all day. She'd come to school in a more outlandish outfit than I'd ever seen her in—a billowing emerald green blouse with some black-and-white checkered pants and huge black spidery earrings.

"Oh, the usual. I got thrown out of drama class today and sent to Mrs. Sheldon's office," Lindsay said matter-of-factly.

I sucked in my breath. I'd never been sent to the principal's office in my whole life.

"Mrs. Sheldon is a real jerk. She said she's going to call my mother," Lindsay muttered. Then she smiled slowly. "But you know what? She won't get hold of anyone. I'll have Sheila pretend that she can't speak English, so she can't give a message. Anyway, I doubt Mother will be home until late tonight."

"Lindsay, can't you just talk to your mom about your drama class? I'd tell my mom, and she'd find a way to help me out," I said softly.

Lindsay's face grew tight. "No," she snapped. "I don't want to talk about it anymore."

When we arrived at the Youth Club, Mom gave me a hug. Then she hugged Lindsay too. I wanted to die. How embarrassing, having your mom hug people all the time.

Lindsay didn't seem to notice. She hugged Mom back. Then Mom pushed Lindsay's hair out of her face and lifted Lindsay's chin with her hand. "You're a little pale," Mom said simply.

I rolled my eyes frantically at Mom. Lindsay was in no mood for criticism today. How could my mom be so stupid?

"I'm fine," said Lindsay and turned away from her.

"Well, you two wait in my office for a minute. I'll see if Ash has cleared the auditorium for you to use today."

I turned to apologize to Lindsay when Mom left the office.

"No big deal," Lindsay said with a shrug. She started flipping idly through the phone-number file on Mom's desk.

"Look here!" she said excitedly, stopping and staring at one of the cards. "It's Mrs. Sheldon's home phone number."

"Yeah, what of it? She and Mom coordinate community work together," I said uneasily. I walked over to the desk, ready to snatch away the card. Something in Lindsay's voice was making my stomach feel tense.

"Just let me jot it down," Lindsay said, grabbing a piece of scratch paper and pen. Hurriedly she scribbled down the number and shoved it into her pocket. Then she started humming under her breath.

"What are you going to do with it?" I asked.

"Oh, nothing," was all she would say.

The rehearsal went okay that afternoon, even though I worried about that phone number. I rehearsed my few lines and only flubbed them a few times. Lindsay taught me this neat trick of saying my lines to the clock in the back of the auditorium. That way, I wouldn't notice all the people in the audience looking at me.

"Very good," called Mrs. Fogarty. "Now let's practice the last song, 'I'm the President of My Very Own Fan Club.' "

Lindsay burst into giggles, and Ash silenced her with a frown.

"I'm sorry I giggled like that," Lindsay apologized sweetly to him during the break. He softened, and even got a canned drink for her. I grew even more cheerful and forgot all about the phone number Lindsay had tucked in her pocket.

It was the first thing I heard about the next morning, though. I found out it was painted in giant letters on the walls of the boys' restroom. Underneath it was the message "For a good time, call Shirley." Lindsay was telling everybody during nutrition break that morning. I didn't say anything to Lindsay about it, but instead sat back quietly and felt sick.

The day went from bad to worse when Ms. Penney came walking up to me. She put her arm around me and tried to talk me into staying with Bev on the project. I gave her some of my best excuses, but I'm not sure she believed me.

"Think about it. You're a sensible person," she said as she walked off.

I wished I wasn't so sensible because I felt that a sensible person would report the business about the phone number to the school officials before Mrs. Sheldon got a lot of crank calls that evening.

I tried to call Lindsay all evening, but I only got Sheila. She said, "I'm es—sorry. I no speak English." That meant Lindsay had gotten to her first. I considered asking Ash to help me figure out how to clean up this mess, but I decided against it. He might tell Mom and get me into more trouble.

The next day, I looked everywhere for Lindsay. But she hadn't come to school. That's it, I decided. I would report the number to Joe, and see if he would keep my secret. Maybe I could help him paint over it after school. But no sooner had I walked into the attendance office than Mrs. Sheldon spotted me. Before I could make a fast getaway, she strode up to me.

"I'm searching for the person responsible for the little telephone fiasco we had yesterday," she said, her mouth set in a tight line. "And I hear someone in your crowd just might be behind it."

I ducked my head, trying not to look Mrs. Sheldon in the eye. I felt bad for the trouble she'd been caused. As far as principals go, she wasn't bad. And I felt rotten that I should have had any part, however small, in the problem.

"I'm sorry. I can't tell you anything," I said, wishing I could tell her how sorry I was.

"Very well then," said Mrs. Sheldon. "We shall meet in my office after school every day this week—starting today—until you decide to tell me who scrawled my phone number for the entertainment of this school. Or perhaps your *friend* will decide to come forward."

Hot tears sprang to my eyes. I wanted to shout, "Not fair!" But I didn't. After all, Mrs. Sheldon was a friend of my mother's. And anyway, I knew that I was somewhat to blame.

But by lunchtime, things really began to heat up. Lori slipped me a note in my locker that said that Lindsay had been caught and that she knew it was me who told. I went to Spanish class with a sick stomach. I chewed the inside of my cheek all period long. Could it be true that Mrs. Sheldon had found out it was Lindsay who'd scribbled her phone number on the boys' room wall?

I had to find Lindsay and explain that I had not leaked a word. I tried to call her at home after school, but Sheila answered. This time, I hung up even before she started talking. Then I reported for my first-ever detention.

My anger at Lindsay grew and grew. She didn't come to school for the rest of the week. No one seemed to want to speak to me. They looked me over the same way they had those first few days of school. I was invisible, or so it seemed. And all the while, I still had to report to detention because Lindsay wouldn't come forward and confess her crime. I cried a lot that week in the safety of my bedroom.

On Monday of next week, Lindsay was back at school. I joined up with the kids on the lawn, waiting for the chance to talk to her alone. I noticed Lori and Maria giving each other these weird looks whenever I said a word. Lindsay seemed to be her usual self, even though by now she was caught for the phone crime and would surely be punished. She just smiled her dazzling smile at me from time to time. And when she showed off a fancy new precision watch her mother had bought for her, she took it off and let me be the first to look at it.

I tried it on and oohed and aahed over it, but my heart wasn't in it. I wished I could get Lindsay alone so we could talk. I gave her frantic eye signals, but she didn't seem to notice. When the bell rang, this tall, dark-haired guy maneuvered over to Lindsay, and he walked her to class. She didn't even try to walk with me. I shrugged and walked to my first period class by myself.

I had just slid into my history seat when Brendan tapped me on the shoulder. "Charlie's dying," he whispered. "Bev sure could have used your help yesterday. Lucky thing I stepped in. I think I know how to save him."

"Huh?" I wanted to ask him more questions, but just then Mr. Shaw started a film and the room grew dark and silent. I just sat feeling alternately miserable and angry. First I thought about Lindsay and how she'd betrayed me. Then I started thinking about how Bev hadn't even called me to tell me Charlie was dying. After all, I was the one who found him. But then another voice reminded me uncomfortably that I'd let Bev down when I'd bailed out of the project in the first place. And I was finding out in a big way that betrayal hurt.

After school, when I got to the Youth Club, I was sure glad to see my mom. Her face was about the only friendly one I'd seen all day— except for all the little kids who were in the *I Love Me* program.

We had only a couple more rehearsals to go until the dress rehearsal. By now the kids knew all the songs. Mrs. Fogarty lip-synced but the kids did the rest. Ash and I stood in the wings and helped prompt just a little. But the kids really knew their parts and didn't really need us anymore. Mom would be happy with the final performance, and knowing that made me feel good.

Afterward, Mrs. Fogarty came up to me and gave me a big hug. "I can't wait for your mom to see the dress rehearsal. You and your brother have done such a good job. Thank you." A happy glow stayed with me all night and almost made me forget all my other problems.

The next morning at school, we had a huge assembly about earthquake safety that lasted until lunch. I closed my eyes during a film that was being shown and started daydreaming about the three-story main building collapsing. Somehow, I'd know just where Lindsay was, and pull her alive and unhurt from the wreckage. She'd be so grateful to me for saving her life, she'd tell Mrs. Sheldon that she had written the phone number in the boys' room. Then Lindsay would apologize to me for letting me serve detention for her.

Then in the final scene of my daydream, Lindsay and Bev would agree to be friends, and we'd all walk into the sunset together, arms linked in friendship.

It was a great daydream, but it was only a daydream. In reality, everything was the same. I'd still have to face the kids who thought I'd turned Lindsay in. I'd have to avoid the library where I would be sure to face an angry Bev. What a mess the Social Survival Guide had gotten me into!

It began to rain in the afternoon. I ran to my locker after the last bell, and took off so I wouldn't run into Lindsay. I didn't want her to come with me to rehearsals and botch up the only thing that was going even halfway well.

I ran all the way to the Youth Club after the bus let me off, but I was still soaked. I felt about as glum as the sky looked. When I ducked inside the front door, I kicked off my soggy sneakers and made my way over to Mom's office.

"Hi, Punkin," she said warmly, smiling at me as I came inside. Then she went back to her computer, frowning at the screen. "These budgets," she said, shaking her head. "We just have to make this *I Love Me* thing a success, or we'll never get the committee to approve a single dime for next year."

I gulped and nodded.

"You look tired. Is something wrong?" Mom asked suddenly. She was giving me one of her "something's up" looks. "Do you want to talk about it?" she asked with a concerned look.

Tears threatened to spill over, but I forced them back. "Nothing's wrong," I said. "I'd better go help paint posters."

I dragged my way to the supply room. Ash was already there, as usual. Newspapers had been spread out all over the floor, and the kids were busily painting. Ash was lettering a poster.

"Let's start getting the hats together," he whispered. Luckily, the rehearsal went better than ever before. The kids behaved like angels. There wasn't a single fight or even a single tear. I was pretty happy by the time we led the tired kids back to their moms.

That evening, I sat upstairs in my bedroom doing homework and wishing Ash would take off somewhere so I could sneak into his room and use his computer. I was having real trouble with this time line my history teacher had assigned us.

Suddenly the phone rang. It was Lindsay, and she was crying.

"What's wrong?" I asked, but hesitated to say much. "Are you upset because you got caught writing the phone number?" I was about to tell her I hadn't turned her in.

"No, it wasn't a big deal. Anyway, my mom got me off," Lindsay sobbed.

"Then what's wrong?" I asked again.

"Everything," Lindsay sobbed. "We've got to talk. You're the only one I can talk to."

"Tell me what's wrong," I said, but Lindsay only sobbed more.

"I'm coming over to your house," I finally said.

"You can't possibly walk in this rain," sobbed Lindsay.

I almost laughed. Lindsay and her horror of walking.

"I'll ask for a ride," I said.

I hung up the phone completely baffled. What could be the matter with Lindsay? Maybe she was sorry about the whole phone number thing and was calling to apologize. I explained about Lindsay's crying and begged Ash for a ride. Surprise of my life—he agreed. Then I asked Mom's permission. She frowned, but said okay.

"I suppose if she's having that big of a problem, she must need your level head," Mom said as she studied my face.

That made me feel pretty warm inside. I mean, sometimes I guess it did come in handy to be the calm, steady type instead of the flashy type who sometimes, well, short-circuited.

"You will call me if it's a big problem," Mom

said. It was nice that she said this as though I had the good sense to do it.

I changed my clothes to a nicer pair of jeans and a warm, fuzzy white sweater. I brushed my hair, and put on some fresh lip gloss. Then I waited by the front door for Ash.

"Bye, Mom," I called and ran out the door.

I ran down the front walk and jumped into Ash's car. Ash turned the radio up loudly, so luckily we didn't have to talk. I didn't want to hear Ash tell me Lindsay was using me again.

Where was she when you were having problems? he'd probably say.

When we drove up Lindsay's driveway, I could see Lindsay standing under the courtyard overhang waiting for me. At least, I noted with relief, she wasn't crying anymore. I climbed out of the car, and Ash said he'd pick me up in an hour. As Lindsay and I went inside the mansion, it hit me how empty that big house was.

"Where's your mother and father?" I asked as we passed a room I assumed to be the library.

"Here," said Lindsay with a small laugh. She pointed to a huge oil portrait of the two of them that was hanging over the enormous fireplace. We stopped so I could get a better look at the imposing picture. There was

Desirée draped in folds of deep blue material. There were sapphires on a huge necklace at her throat. A large blue ring flashed on one of her fingers. Lindsay's dad was your basic tall, blond, and handsome type.

I let out a low whistle. "Wow," I said. Lindsay didn't say anything.

"Come on," she finally said. "Let's go up to my room where we can talk."

As soon as we got to Lindsay's room, I expected she would start talking. And maybe she'd tell me why she had been crying. But she did neither of those things. She simply turned on her huge stereo system with speakers blaring from all over the place and started dancing. Wildly. Her hair flowed all over the place, and before too long, she had really worked up a sweat. I sat on the flowered comforter on her bed and watched in a weird fascination.

She never said a word about why she was crying or why she had called me. And of course she didn't thank me for dropping everything to come over.

Later that night, I sat in my room with the radio playing low. I thought about a lot of things. Like popularity. And friendship. The true meaning of friendship. I also thought about my parents and how much I loved them.

It was a lot to think about.

Ten

THE next morning, I woke up with a funny feeling. It wasn't a bad feeling, but it wasn't a good feeling. It was the feeling that something was about to change in a big way for me today.

Bev and I saw each other at the bus stop, but we didn't speak to each other. Bev pretended to read a book. I pretended I was listening to the talk going on around me. I found myself wishing I could say some magic words to Bev, and we'd be friends again. But there didn't seem to be any point in wishing.

The minute we got to school, I headed toward the lawn where I knew I'd find Lindsay. I wanted to see how she was after last night. Maybe today she'd want to talk.

She was hanging around, laughing with her group as usual. The dark-haired guy who'd walked her to class the other day stood next to her. When she saw me, she kind of nodded her head and continued chatting with the others—as though last night had never happened.

"Are you okay?" I finally managed to whisper just before the first-period bell rang.

Lindsay's face was a complete blank. "What? Of course I'm okay."

"Well, I thought after last night—you're sure you're okay?"

"What's the matter? Don't I look okay? Hey, guys, Lisa here wants to know if I'm okay!" Lindsay giggled hysterically. She looked right into the eyes of the guy. I wondered for a second who he was, but I had that feeling again that I'd seen him somewhere before. Then the laughter of the group interrupted my wondering.

I could feel my cheeks burn. What was going on? Last night Lindsay had called me crying. She had seemed on the edge of sharing something secret with me. Then today it was like we were strangers. I wondered if the dark-haired guy had something to do with the whole thing. Suddenly, I realized he was Kevin, the guy from drama class—the one Lindsay had called stupid. Only now she wasn't looking at him like she thought he was stupid. She looked at him the way she'd once looked at Ash. I felt cold inside.

"I need to talk with you," I said while the others turned to gather up their books.

"About what?" Lindsay said lightly.

Then I did something I'd never dared to do to Lindsay before. I grabbed her arm. "Come with me," I said. "We need to talk."

"About what?"

I kept her walking until we were out in the parking lot beyond where the latecomers were still trickling in. Then I turned to face her.

"Look, what's going on here?" I demanded. "Last night—"

"*I do not want to talk about it,*" she said with her icy-cold stare.

"Well, I do," I persisted. "Why were you crying last night? You need to talk with somebody. Look, I care about you." I pleaded with my eyes.

Lindsay's eyes were cold and blank.

"People don't care about me. You don't care about me. I don't care about you. You're a nothing," she said meanly. "And you know something else? Your precious big brother isn't so hot either. I mean, only a loser would wipe little kids' noses the way he does. Kevin's definitely more my type."

I stood there, my mind trying to do something with all the emotions that flooded through me just then. It was hard because there were too many of them, and they came all at once. Confusion. Fear. Guilt. Frustration. Finally, anger.

"Fine," I said, feeling myself grow angrier by the minute. "We won't talk about last night. Or Kevin. But I do want to ask you one question. Why did you let me take the heat for the phone number and sit there in detention for a week?"

Lindsay gave me another one of her icy-cold stares. "Better you than me."

Then she turned and walked off. I stood there stunned, like I'd been slapped in the face. Then very slowly I started walking to class. And do you know what? I realized I wasn't even angry anymore. Only sad.

But that feeling soon took a nosedive to misery by the time I got to my first-period class. I'd lost a friend. I'd lost my chance at popularity. I'd lost a lot of things.

I stayed at home the next day with a cold that brought a heavy-duty case of the sniffles. Unfortunately, that gave me a lot of time to think about a lot of things. Maybe Lindsay had never really been a friend at all. Lori, Maria, and the rest weren't friends either. My mom and Ash had been right. I'd missed out on understanding popularity because I'd believed the Social Survival Guide was really the answer.

Because I was sick for two days, I also missed the dress rehearsal for the *I Love Me* program—my last chance to say my lines before I'd have to deliver them to an audience.

The afternoon of the second day of my sneezy misery, Ash bounded by my room and stuck his head in the door.

"Hey, are you tired of faking it yet?" he teased. I sneezed three times in a row as an answer.

"Whoa, I think I'd better stay away from you, Typhoid Mary," he said. He stood in the doorway, and I listened as he told me how great the dress rehearsal had gone that afternoon. It was only called a dress rehearsal, he said, because the kids wouldn't get their costumes until the actual performance.

"Mrs. Fogarty insists that half of the kids will trash their T-shirts completely if they get them before the big night," Ash said with a laugh. "Well, I'm out of here. I don't want to get sick. Next week's the state meet."

The next day, I still didn't feel well enough to go to school, but I did start to feel bored. I wished I had some new mystery books from the library so I had something to read. I was even starting to miss doing homework. Late that afternoon, I took a warm bath, got dressed and went downstairs. No one was in the family room, so I flipped on the TV. I started to watch *Treasure Trove* on TV, but seeing Desirée displaying the attractions of a set of trash cans for every day of the week made me think of Lindsay. I sure didn't want to do that, so I shut off the TV.

Just then, I heard a knock at the front door. When I opened the door, I saw Ms. Penney standing there holding a huge Indian purse and a couple of folders.

"Hi, Lisa," she greeted me. "How are you feeling?"

A-choo! "Better," I managed, after blowing my nose. "I'll be back at school probably tomorrow."

"Great. I thought you might be worried about falling behind on your science work, so I thought I'd stop by and drop these off for you." Ms. Penney handed me a manila folder.

"Thanks," I said. I was impressed. There weren't too many teachers who would take the time to do something like this for a sick student.

"Well, I just didn't want to see you falling behind," Ms. Penney added. She fumbled with her purse for a minute like she wanted to say something else.

"Uh, you know, Ms. Penney, I hope you're not mad at me about that 'Fun with Fungus' project," I said shyly.

"Oh, no. Disappointed, of course, but from what I understand from Bev and Brendan, Charlie's past danger now. And since it's only a week until the projects are due in for judging, I don't think anything else will go wrong." She smiled prettily at me. "All's well that ends well. See you in school."

Oddly enough, that wasn't exactly what I wanted to hear. I guessed I'd hoped she would tell me that Bev couldn't do the project without me. And that she was insisting I be back on the project. *But real life doesn't work that way,* I thought to myself.

I moped all afternoon until Mom and Dad came home from work and fussed over me and, in general, cheered me up.

I came to school the next day armed with a box of tissues. Bev and I were still total strangers. As soon as I stepped off the bus, I spotted Lindsay and Kevin and the group in their usual spot. Deliberately, I walked past them. Lindsay didn't even glance at me. I knew it was all over.

Right after nutrition break, I went to my locker and opened it. Bev had cleared her stuff out. I guess she was sharing with someone else now. Our Social Survival Guide was sitting there on top of some other books. I picked it up and opened it, then I shredded those rotten notes and threw them into the trash barrel.

I felt happier than I had in days.

The next day was the day of the program. Mom, Dad, Ash, and I were at the Youth Club. Mrs. Fogarty, two mothers, and I were assigned to the folding tables to check out costumes to the kids. Since the costumes were all alike this year—yellow T-shirts that said Hug Me in huge letters—it wasn't that big of a deal. Last year, we'd had to do traffic-light-colored T-shirts for the Safety Kid program. We'd had to give red to the little girls, yellow to the little boys, and green to the bigger kids. You wouldn't believe the tears! Some kids wanted to wear the same color as a brother or sister. Others wanted a different color from a brother or sister. I tell you it was a real mess. But this year, it went smoothly.

I hung around for a while longer, helping Ash and my dad set up some of the cardboard scenery.

"All done, Lisa?" asked Dad. "The kids aren't due here until five, so why don't you run home and shower? Just be back here in an hour."

I was glad to escape. Sitting around with nothing to do just made my stomach do handsprings. I ran home, saying my single line to myself at least two hundred times.

After my shower, I changed into my yellow T-shirt and a jeans skirt, which was the rest of the costume. I was just combing my hair when I heard a familiar voice coming up from the street. Bev! I ran to my window that faced the street and was just about to throw it open to yell "Hi!" But that's before I saw that she wasn't alone. She was with Brendan.

She was laughing wildly at something he'd said, doubled over holding her stomach. Brendan had his hands in his pockets and was smiling at her. The sun was glinting off his dark brown hair, and they looked so . . . I don't know. Well, *happy*. The handsprings in my stomach turned into furious jumping jacks. I turned away from the window and sat on my bed, certain I was going to get sick again.

So now Bev liked Brendan! And after all that time I felt so bad about sneaking around trying to get Ash and Lindsay together! I picked up a stuffed giraffe I keep on my bed and threw it at the wall. But as I watched it thud, I remembered that only a few days ago, I had realized that *I* was the one who messed up my best friendship. Not Bev—me. I toyed with the friendship bracelet I was still wearing. Well, it was too late. I had made Bev mad at me, and there was nothing I could do to change it. I'd been a real idiot dumping a good friend like Bev for an industrial-strength creep like Lindsay. Maybe Bev would never speak to me again anyway, but tomorrow I was going to apologize to her. That at least would make me feel better.

I stood up and finished getting ready. I'd have to hurry. I put on a little bit of Mom's blush so I wouldn't look washed out under the stage lights. I dabbed on some of her face powder so my skin wouldn't look shiny. Then I put on my usual mascara and lip gloss. There, I didn't look so bad. So maybe I'd let down my friends, but there was no way I was going to let down my family—or myself.

Feeling better by the time I arrived at the Youth Club, I stepped inside the auditorium.

"Ready to flub your big line?" Ash teased. I punched him in the arm.

"I'm *not* going to flub it," I retorted.

Ash, Ryan, and I hung out in the wings while Mom and Dad dashed home to shower and change. Ash had already pulled on his yellow T-shirt with some clean jeans. We sat on some packing crates offstage. Ash and Ryan talked about their upcoming state meet. I could tell Ash was nervous too, and that amazed me. I mean, my oh-so-cool brother, *nervous*?

Somehow that made me feel less nervous.

Pretty soon Mom and Dad were back. Little by little, the kids and their parents started trickling in. I was in charge of corralling them into the wings. There, Ash and Mrs. Fogarty checked their costumes to make sure everything was okay. Most of the kids were excited, but one little girl burst into tears and had to be taken back to her mother. I brought the little girl out to the lobby where the parents were gathered for coffee and hors d'oeuvres. Soon other people from the community started pouring in. The lights were dimmed.

"Wow," Ash hissed as he peeked around the curtain into the darkened auditorium. "The whole place is full."

Suddenly it was time. "Places, everybody." Mrs. Fogarty scurried in and clapped her hands. The spotlight came on.

Even the kids were quiet for a moment, except for some rustling and stifled giggling. I took a deep breath. In a couple of minutes, I would be on that stage. But somehow, I knew I could do it. So maybe I wasn't glamorous and maybe I didn't have movie-star blood running in me. But I did have sensible blood in me. And I was finding out more and more that that counted for a lot of things. I took another deep breath.

The next minute, I was out there. The lone spotlight was on me.

"Ladies and gentlemen, the Youth Club Tot Singers are happy to present the *I Love Me* program. And you're invited to hug along!"

Everyone laughed, and I drew a rather shaky breath as I stepped back into the lineup. I hadn't stuttered or forgotten a single word! Then the lights flooded the stage and the children ran on, screaming and hugging themselves, but finding their right places immediately. Ash threw me a brilliant smile as he raised his hands for the first dance movements.

And while we were singing about loving ourselves just the way we were, it hit me. I did like me the way I was. I looked at the joyful five-year-old faces around me. They were just being themselves and they were happy. And I didn't need to act or look like someone else to be a better person. I was me! And I liked me! I gave myself a tight hug as the curtain went down to thundering applause.

There was chaos for a minute, then Ash came over and hugged me. So did a zillion little kids, and I hugged them back. Then I ran over and hugged Mrs. Fogarty. Then my mom came backstage and hugged us all. You never saw so much hugging in your whole life!

127

"That was wonderful!" Mom said, her eyes bright as high beams. "You all did such a great job!"

"Will you get the money you need for your budget?" Ash asked in his straight-out way.

She ruffled his head like a little boy even though he was almost six feet tall. "I almost don't care about all that right now. But yes, I think so. I think the community realizes how much we need programs like these."

"Yoo-hoo," came a voice from behind me. I whirled around. It was Bev—with Brendan. I stood there rooted to the floor a minute, not knowing what to say. But then I realized it didn't matter if Bev and Brendan liked each other. I began to feel good realizing that fight or no fight, Bev still liked me enough to come after all.

It was Brendan who spoke first. "You were great, Lisa," he said. Then he did something which amazed me. *He* gave me a hug. I almost died on the spot. "Bev told me she was coming to watch you tonight, so I asked if I could come see you, too. I mean, I wanted to see you." He stammered, looked away, then blushed.

I froze for a second as a blinding thought hit me. Brendan wasn't interested in Bev—he was interested in me!

Then Bev and I looked at each other. A zillion things passed between us those few seconds. Then, I don't know who hugged who first, but we both hugged for a long time.

Finally, she drew back. "I know this isn't exactly the best time to tell you this. But Brendan and I have a confession to make," she said. "We also came to ask your help on the science project. Charlie's still not doing too well."

"But Ms. Penney told me—" I began.

Brendan held up a hand. "I know," he said quietly. "That's what we told her. The thing is, he's looking awful. Dried out. I gave him water. It didn't help."

I burst into happy laughter. Not because Charlie was dying, but because Bev still needed me. So did Brendan. Besides, I had an idea that just might save Charlie. But all I said was, "You're right. This isn't exactly the time or place to talk about fungus."

Bev and I broke into furious giggles. It was Bev who caught her breath first. "I'd better go tell my dad where I am. He drove us, and he's up in the lobby waiting for us," she said.

"Ask him to join us for a celebratory ice-cream sundae," boomed my dad as he came forward from the wings.

"Guess what? Brendan told me he thinks

you're totally neat," Bev whispered as we moved out of earshot.

I smiled, and didn't say a word. Then the two of us ran up the aisle just like little kids. I didn't care who saw us or how uncool we acted. Bev and I were friends again!

Eleven

WELL, that was it. I was out of the popular crowd and totally into the science project again. It felt great. I realized I had a knack for making friends after all. I simply made a point to talk with people—not just sit back and wait for them to notice me. And with my best friendship on track, I felt better than ever about everything.

Charlie felt better than ever these days as well . . . thanks to my theory. You see, I did a little studying of my own. And I found out that technically Charlie was a slime mold, and that some scientists classified him as an animal. Bev had been treating him as a plant and figured he could just live off air and water. But he needed the diet of any healthy animal. So I sprinkled his plate with vegetable scrapings. And by the night before the fair, he was back to his flourishing fuchsia self.

The day of the fair, Bev and Brendan piled into our station wagon with my family. Brendan sat on one side balancing a huge plastic container that held Charlie, who was still perched on his microwave plate. Bev sat on the other side with her feet resting on the pegboard exhibit. The rest of the stuff for our exhibit was stuffed in the trunk. I sat on the bump in the middle, squeezed between the two of them. Ash and Ryan sat in the backseat.

Bev pretended she wasn't excited to be in the same car as Ash. And I pretended not to notice that Brendan did some pretty slick maneuvers so he could sit next to me. Actually, this was no time to think about guys at all. Charlie and the blue ribbon at the science fair were the important things right now.

"Think you'll be comfortable sitting like that all the way to Disneyland?" my dad asked, eyeing us all dubiously.

Ash and Ryan didn't hear because they were both plugged into headphones.

"Yeah," Bev and I chorused.

Then my parents turned on the radio to this really dippy station as soon as we got on the freeway. I rolled my eyes at Bev. "Isn't this the worst music?" I groaned in a low voice so my parents wouldn't hear.

"How can you worry about the music at a time like this?" Bev hissed severely. She gave me the Stern Look, and I decided right then that one day Bev would make a great study-hall teacher. She had that Stern Look down pat.

"Oh, stop worrying, Bev," said Brendan. "Thanks to Lisa and her vegetable theory, Charlie's in tip-top shape. He'll wow those judges. I just know he will. So start thinking about where you'll hang that blue ribbon."

This time it was Bev's turn to roll her eyes. "I'm sick of you going on and on about how Lisa saved this project," she said in a teasing tone. "Don't forget that Charlie managed quite nicely with me for a while."

"You just attract the lowlifes," Ash cracked from the back. He'd pulled off his headset and leaned forward to thump Bev on the head.

Bev blushed a deep red that almost matched the color of the blouse she was wearing. "Oh, go veg out with your headphones," she said, straightening her shiny hair.

We joked around for most of the rest of the trip, which helped Bev and me forget our worries for a while. When we arrived at the Disneyland hotel, Bev and I ran up ahead to find out where we had to check in with our exhibit. Brendan stayed behind with my family to help carry Charlie and the other stuff.

The place was jammed. "Look at all these people," I breathed. "Do you think they're all here just for the science fair?"

"I don't know," Bev said in a fearful whisper.

Both of us stared as we walked through the elegant lobby of the hotel. We passed a waterway where some people were paddleboating. Pretty soon we noticed signs that led us through more doors to a huge banquet room.

"Look. There's Ms. Penney," I said, pointing just inside the door. Ms. Penney was dressed in a pretty red shirtdress. She was standing next to a gray-haired man dressed in a suit.

"Oh, Bev, Lisa. There you are. We've got plenty of time to set up your exhibit," she said. "Oh, by the way, this is my husband, Jon Penney."

I stuck out my hand politely and he shook it. It was kind of weird. I mean, you don't think of teachers as having husbands and stuff.

Already, there were lots of kids we knew from school setting up their projects. But we didn't bother walking around just yet to check out the others' setups. We had work of our own to do.

Mom and Dad, followed by Ash, Ryan, and

Brendan came into the room, loaded down with everything.

"We'll meet you at the paddleboats when you're finished here," Dad said. "Don't forget all the students have to clear out during the judging."

"C'mon," Ash said to Ryan. "Let's hit the rides."

They all left, and Bev, Brendan, and I set to work. We'd practiced setting up the whole thing and taking it down so there would be no surprises on the day of the fair. It was Bev who insisted on that. That's a scientific mind for you.

Forty-five minutes later, the whole thing was erected. Bev stepped back. "Don't you think Charlie might be getting too big for that plate?" she said with a frown.

"Don't even think of moving him now," I gasped. "Charlie could get messed up, and we don't want that."

"There's nothing worse than a fungal bungle," said Brendan with a huge grin.

"Oh, stop it," Bev said. "Who needs a wise guy at a time like this?"

I looked over at Brendan, and a small wave of guilt hit me. If it hadn't been for his partner bailing out of their goldfish project, he'd have a chance at the blue ribbon himself. As it was, he could only watch everyone else get a chance at the glory.

Then all three of us stepped back and eyed the exhibit critically. I had to admit, it looked great. Ash had helped with the lettering that spelled out "Fun With Fungus" at the top center portion of the pegboard. Bev's carefully copied charts were mounted at the right. I'd written out an explanation of fungi's place in the food chain, and the type of fungus—slime mold—that Charlie was. I also had written a few sentences on how I'd found Charlie, though I didn't mention that I'd found him in Ash's room. Ash would have killed me. Besides, I hadn't even told Ash. "Come on," I said, grabbing Bev's arm. "Let's go see the rest of the exhibits before the judges get here."

"I'm not sure I'll be able to stand it if anyone else's exhibit is better than ours," said Bev.

"No one's could be better," Brendan said. I threw him a grateful smile. We were going to need all the votes of confidence we could get.

As we walked through the room checking out all the other projects, I was filled with a warm sense of belonging. I mean, wow! Who knew? One of these days somebody in this room might grow up and do something really important like discover a cure for cancer or something. It might even be me!

I always knew I had a sensible mind, I'd say.

After a while, the judges came in, and we were all shooed from the room. We met my mom and dad and then we all took off for Disneyland. Of course, we totally forgot about the science fair for the rest of the day. Ash, Ryan, Bev, Brendan, and I took off immediately for Space Mountain. After that, we hit the Matterhorn at least three times.

Brendan took me on the flying jets in Tomorrowland, and I didn't even mind when he kept the ship at the highest setting the whole ride. Of course, Bev was dying to go to the Haunted House, so we managed to squeeze that in, too. Then we had to start heading back to the Disneyland Hotel to wash up and get ready for the banquet. I sure didn't want to leave Disneyland just yet, but I was getting pretty anxious about the awards again.

Bev and I had a hotel room to ourselves. Ash, Ryan, and Brendan had one together a couple of doors down next to my parents. We waved good-bye to the guys and went to our room to get ready.

After we showered, we changed into our dresses. I'd chosen a tea-length mint-colored chiffon. It had a low neckline. I put on a thick silver chain and some silver earrings. Then I studied my eyes against the green color of my outfit.

"Does it make my eyes look green?" I asked hopefully. Bev looked at me in the mirror and shook her head.

"Sorry, but your eyes are gray," she said firmly. "But you look great. Now help me with this zipper."

Bev had chosen a short, lacy pink dress and some pearls that looked very real. She looked awfully cute in it, and I told her so. We carefully applied our mascara, and then Bev triumphantly produced some perfume which we sprayed liberally.

"Done," Bev said, taking one last satisfied look in the mirror.

A little while later, we met Mom and Dad in the lobby.

"You two look dazzling," my dad said when we made our entrance into the lobby. "Absolutely, undeniably dazzling."

"Oh, Dad, stop it," I muttered. Bev turned red, but I could tell she was pleased.

"I can almost stand looking at you," Ash said as he came through the glass doors, followed by Ryan and Brendan.

I shook my head. Brothers. But then he took Bev's arm and Brendan took mine and they led us to the banquet room. Ryan complained noisily about being the odd man out, but no one listened to him.

I could hardly believe my eyes when we stepped into the banquet room. I mean, it looked so important. The tables were set with pink tablecloths and glasses that looked like crystal. The judges' table had a podium with a microphone on it.

Pretty soon, the place was packed. Ms. Penney motioned our family over to a table near the front of the room. I sat carefully, hoping I wouldn't do something dumb like knock over my water glass. Bev sat on one side of me, and Brendan sat on the other.

"Look," Bev whispered excitedly. "Our names are in the program."

Wow! Last year's science fair banquet where we'd won the red ribbon hadn't been nearly as fancy as this. I felt very important and grown up sitting here. I tossed my hair back like I'd seen Lindsay do so many times. I wondered what she was doing right now.

But I didn't have time to think about her for very long because someone tapped a spoon on a glass to get everyone's attention. The master of ceremonies introduced the panel of judges. He then explained about regions, and said the usual stuff about how he wished every exhibit could win. He seemed to talk forever.

"Hurry up already," I grumbled to myself. I couldn't stand waiting any longer.

Brendan gave me a thumbs-up sign. Bev and I held our breath as he started to read the names of the winning entries, starting with the high schools. The emcee must have read a zillion names. Then we had to wait while each group went up to receive their ribbons. Bev kept kicking me under the table, and I kicked her back. Finally he got to the middle schools.

"And now, for Region Seven. The blue ribbon for first prize goes to Foothill Middle School—the 'Fun With Fungus' project by Lisa Halloran and Bev Hansen!"

"Way to go!" yelled Ash loudly, and the whole room burst into laughter.

Bev and I jumped up and gave each other a quick hug. Bev started to sit back down, but I grabbed her arm. "Come on! We have to go up there and get our ribbons," I hissed as Bev hung back. Her eyes grew wide and frightened, but she walked up front with me.

We got our blue ribbon. I leaned into the microphone after shaking the emcee's hand.

"I want to thank lots of people, like our parents and Ms. Penney, our science teacher. But most of all, I want to thank my best friend, Beverly Hansen," I said, turning to Bev.

Then Bev did something I never believed possible. She leaned toward the microphone and croaked out, "And I want to thank my best friend, Lisa Halloran."

We walked back to the table together, loving every minute of the applause.

After dinner, the dancing began. First I danced with my dad and then with Ash.

"You're okay for a little sister," Ash said as we moved to the music. "You've got it over girls like Lindsay any day of the week."

I smiled, but a little sadly. My mind slipped away from the science fair for a moment as I thought about Lindsay. I was sorry things had turned out so rotten with her. But I'd learned some important things. Things I'd be in no danger of forgetting for a while. I only hoped that one day she'd learn some things too, from someone she cared about.

"May I cut in?"

That jolted me back to the science fair. It was Brendan, and he wanted to dance with me. Ash broke away, and pulled Bev onto the dance floor. The fast rock beat I'd been dancing to with Ash turned into a slow dance, and Brendan put his arms around my waist.

As I leaned my cheek against Brendan's shoulder, I was blissfully aware that right now, just for this minute, I was 100 percent happy.

Happy that Bev and I had won the blue ribbon. Happy that Brendan seemed to like me. Happy for Bev that she was dancing with Ash. Happy that Bev and I were still best friends forever. Happy to have my family. But most of all, I was happy just being me!

About the Author

KARLE DICKERSON is the managing editor of a young women's fashion and beauty magazine based in Southern California. She lives with her husband and numerous animals, including a horse, a Welsh pony, three cats, a dog, and two hermit crabs.

"I first decided to be a writer when I was 10 years old and had a poem published in the local paper," she says. "I wrote almost every day in a journal from that day on. I still use some of the growing-up situations I jotted down then for my novel ideas and magazine articles."

Mrs. Dickerson spends her spare time at Stonehouse Farms, a Southern California equestrian center she and her husband formed with some friends. She says, "I love to ride my horse around the ranch and people-watch. It seems this is when I come up with some of my best ideas!"

The author adds that while she was growing up, she was lucky enough to have a best friend like Bev, who was able to forgive and forget. "In fact, we're still best friends to this day!"